CONTENTS

ON HORROR

SIMON STRANTZAS

FEAR WITHOUT THE THREAT

THE DREAM SEQUENCE is one of those techniques that is closely linked to Horror. While it appears in other genres of fiction, I'd argue the preponderance of occurrences are within horror narratives. Horror can't get enough of the dream sequence, and I'm not convinced it's always in the genre's best interest.

Before you tear out your hair and dash off an angry letter to the editor let me assure you that despite my apparent distain for the dream sequence, I've written my fair share of them. Albeit begrudgingly. And, perhaps, lazily. Because, yes, I think the dream sequence is often a lazy short-cut in Horror. And I suspect that's the reason its use is so popular.

To reiterate: I'm talking about the dream sequence—a short moment of surreality within a longer more grounded narrative—and not oneiric fiction, where the entire narrative is intentionally told through a surrealistic lens. The latter is almost a different genre (or at least subgenre) from Horror, and doesn't necessarily suffer from the same issues.

When it comes to non-oneiric Horror, the dream sequence is often used to achieve one or more of the following: the early introduction of horrific elements when they don't yet fit; the foreshadowing of later frightening or revelatory events to lend them more narrative weight; the injection of dread before anything dreadful has had an opportunity to occur.

A typical narrative follows a linear structure (even if told non-linearly): first, characters and setting are established; then a disruption occurs that propels the protagonist into looking for a solution; finally, the protagonist confronts the disruption and is changed by it. Because Horror stories (besides being tales of fear) are narratives of mystery, the writer must drive their characters to investigate the horrific disruption without them facing a threat that grows so terrifying that any reasonable person would flee.

A popular way to solve this "reasonable person problem" is to isolate the characters, either physically (the remote cabin, the washed-out bridge, the neighbours who've gone home for the summer) or emotionally (the break-up, the abusive parent, the mental illness). By preventing the characters from leaving their situation, the writer can increase both the threat and the fear in conjunction, knowing the characters have no choice but to confront the oncoming horror in some fashion. But where isolation isn't possible, writers will often rely on the dream sequence to introduce the horror and avoid the resistance that might be expected from a reasonable person.

What makes the dream sequence so irresistible is its versatility. It can be inserted to energize a story should it begin to slow, and it offers the writer the opportunity to introduce fantastical elements, or build a dreadful atmosphere, or present something exaggeratedly horrific, all while providing the characters with an experience that can be disregarded as an immaterial figment. The presentation of fear without the inherent threat.

I suppose my issue is that it all seems too easy. A cop-out. A lazy way of conveying information to the reader—whether it's about plot or atmosphere—because finding a more organic way to introduce these ideas (while also contending with the "reasonable person") is too challenging. Finding ways to make characters willingly wade further into, not out of, horror requires rethinking what motivates people to put their lives at potential risk and determining how those motivations can be manipulated to further mire characters in something dangerous that they have no control over. But putting that work in can only help to strengthen characters and increase their complexity. Ultimately, it can only make for better, more emotionally resonant stories.

But we needn't abandon all that the dream sequence has to offer. I'd like to see more stories that take the fantastical strengths of the dream sequence—the disjointed narrative, the wrongness, the confusion and strangeness—and remake them as literal. Integrate them into the story as one might have previously done with a dream, but instead have those events *actually occur*. Take, for example, the hallucinatory finale of Ben Wheatley's film, *In the Earth*. During a spore-induced drug trip (which is, for all intents and purposes, a dream sequence) the characters end up in communion with a greater power. The scene retains the strange quality of a dream while the events that transpire truly happen. Indeed, not only do they happen through this transformative state, but it's implied *this is the only way communication can occur*. Thus, the two issues of the dream sequence—its lack of true occurrence and affect—are resolved. Let's have more of this: the character who, while awake, finds themselves suddenly on an endless street; the grotesque laughing faces that hang in the air and share real space with the protagonist. Let's make the nightmares real, and then have our characters contend with those nightmares. When dreams are not dreams at all, the horrors they contain are arguably more affecting and far less escapable even where isolation is impossible.

Or maybe there are other solutions that can provide those things we get from a dream sequence without resorting to the lack of material affect the dream sequence brings. Because that may be the ultimate problem with the dream sequence: they're inconsequential. They lack power because they aren't real. Even when we load them with meaning and portance, they ultimately are just dreams and can't hurt our characters. At best, their affect is metatextual, intended more for the writer to explain the story than for the characters who suffer through it. I described the dream sequence earlier as not raising the threat, but it's worse than that. The dream sequence doesn't even keep the threat in check; it deflates it. The dream sequence robs any power the story might have during those few minutes it appears because the moment means nothing. It didn't happen. It isn't real.

And Horror should be real, shouldn't it? It should at least feel that way. Not necessarily in the sense of subject matter, but in the sense of what it means. There should be truth to Horror, to every part of it. It should all mean something, and I'm not sure the addition of a dream sequence always gets us there.

GREY'S GROTESQUERIES

ORRIN GREY

PARALLEL EVOLUTION: A TALE OF TWO MUCK MONSTERS

AMONG FILM NERDS, there is a phenomenon that is routinely discussed. You're probably familiar with it: the situation where we get two movies with similar loglines in a single year, such as 1998, which gave us both *Deep Impact* and *Armageddon*, or 2006, which saw dueling Victorian stage magician movies hitting theaters in the form of *The Prestige* and *The Illusionist*.

The reasons for this kind of parallel evolution are many and varied and not really what we're here to discuss. Instead, we're here to explore possibly the most famous and enduring of all instances of this phenomenon, which took place not on the big screen but in the pages of comic books in the 1970s.

Even in this age of Google and Wikipedia, where boundless knowledge (much of it wrong) rests at the tips of our fingers, there is much confusion and misunderstanding about the origins of Swamp Thing (created for DC Comics by Len Wein and Bernie Wrightson) and Man-Thing (created for Marvel by Roy Thomas, Gerry Conway, and Gray Morrow), with most people assuming that one is a rip-off of the other. Oddly enough, this doesn't seem to be the case.

While Swamp Thing is certainly the more successful of the pair, having starred in a variety of acclaimed comic books (including a run by Alan Moore which ranks among the greatest classics of the form) as well as two movies and a pair of TV series, Man-Thing (who bears a more unintentionally humorous moniker) actually beat his DC doppelganger to the stands by a month.

So, how did the unlikely duo creep from the muck? To trace the origins of these two startlingly similar swamp monsters, we have to go all the way back to 1940 and a short story by sci-fi legend Theodore Sturgeon. The tale in question, simply titled "It," first appeared in the August 1940 issue of the sci-fi pulp *Unknown,* and proceeded to create the template for the many muck monsters that would follow.

This is interesting for a number of reasons, not least because, when it comes to monsters as powerfully iconic as these, we can rarely point to a single source and say, "This. It all started here." Bram Stoker's seminal novel may have popularized the modern conception of the vampire, but he was drawing from a vast wellspring of folklore and even previous fiction. With muck monsters—at least, the type epitomized by our two unlikely heroes—there seems to be virtually no precedent before Sturgeon's story, though even it has precursors, such as the "green monkey" in H. R. Wakefield's "The Red Lodge" from 1928, as Scott Nicolay points out in one of his excellent Stories from the Borderland blogs.

I said that "It" established the template, but what *is* that template? In *Swampmen,* an installment of the periodical *Comic Book Creator* focused exclusively on "Muck-Monsters and Their Makers," the form is defined as "those reanimated corpses taking on the physical characteristics of swampland. That is, creatures of once living and breathing human flesh but, through whatever horrid process, they are transformed from man into monster, now composed of mud, debris, and muck 'n' mire, and often great strength."

In part, it is that human corpse—and, sometimes, human consciousness—at the heart of the muck monster that sets it apart from a variety of plant-based creeps who have haunted the pages of comics and books, and the screens of multiplexes, for years. In Sturgeon's original story, the body belongs to a fellow by the name of Roger Kirk, but the creature that emerges bears none of his personality. That changes as the various swamp creatures emerge from the muck in comic books through the 1970s.

The first such beast shows up much earlier, though, hot on the heels of Sturgeon's story. In the December 1942 issue of *Air Fighter Comics* we are introduced to the Heap, the first of the muck monsters to shamble onto the four-color pages of comic books, where they would enjoy their greatest success. Initially, the Heap was a German flying ace named Baron Emmelmann who crashed his plane into a marsh and emerged as a white-maned swamp creature who sucks the blood of hapless farm animals through prominent fangs.

Over more than a decade of subsequent issues, the Heap rose from throwaway monster to one of the series' most popular characters, with backup stories in the newly retitled *Airboy* comic series that often featured on the cover, sometimes even pushing the title character off entirely. The design of the Heap evolved, too, with the fangs dropping away, his shaggy coat changing color, and his eventual, distinctive "carrot" nose showing up.

That nose is significant to where we're going next, which is not to the *Swamp Thing* and *Man-Thing* comics quite yet but, instead, to *Dungeons & Dragons*. While the roleplaying game first appeared in 1974 —three years after both Swamp Thing and Man-Thing made their debuts—the classic D&D equivalent of a muck monster, the delightfully-named "shambling mound," didn't show up until around 1977, with the publication of the first *Monster Manual*. When it did, though, with art by David C. Sutherland III, it looked an awful lot like the Heap—and even kept his carrot nose!

While the shambling mound may not technically fit our muck monster criteria, being birthed not from a human cadaver but when, according to the 5th edition of the *Monster Manual*, "lightning or fey magic invigorates an otherwise ordinary swamp plant," the shared creative DNA is obvious.

Long before the shambling mound first, well, shambled into the pages of the *Monster Manual*, however, the two most famous incarnations of the muck monster had already appeared in the pages of *House of Mystery* (Swamp Thing) and *Savage Tales* (Man-Thing) in June and May of 1971, respectively. Man-Thing, in particular, borrowed the Heap's root-like nose to create a striking face design, one that would be echoed again by D&D in their LJN toy line released in 1983, where the shambling mound figure "may as well be a Man-Thing toy," as Stu Horvath writes at the Vintage RPG blog.

There's no evidence that the creators of either creature knew of the development of the other, though all involved were likely aware of the

Heap and probably even Sturgeon's oft-reprinted story. That two such iconic creatures could crawl forth from the muck not only independent of one-another but within a month may strain credulity, but it's part of what makes the phenomenon so fascinating, even after all these years...

IN THE DEAD OF THE WOOD

WILLIAM CURNOW

THERE'S sickness in this house. The baby's been off her food, griping for days, and no one knows what's wrong with her. The doctor's been and gone, for all the good that did.

There are arguments. A simmering atmosphere like a saucepan boiling dry. The children are always in the way. They want to draw; no, they want to watch TV but there's nothing good on; no, they want to go outside but it's too cold. They fight, they bicker. A china ballerina gets knocked off the mantelpiece and smashes. The baby wakes, bawling.

"Enough!" stepmother snaps. "If you want to be helpful you can go and check on Granny."

"Not Granny," they chorus, united in dismay.

"You know how lonely it gets out there. She'll be pleased to see you. Go on; no, don't moan—it won't take long. You can be back in time to do your homework, back before it gets dark. You're big enough to do this now. You must shoulder your responsibilities."

They think of Granny's house, deep in the woods.

"We hate going there," they say, listing objections, looking for a way out.

"It's always freezing."

"She never has the heating on."

"It's not even as if she gives us nice things to eat after we've come such a long way."

"No cakes or buns."

"Just stale crusts."

Stepmother brushes the protests aside. Granny must be checked on.

"I'll pack you a basket to take for her."

"Do we really have to?" big sister asks.

"Yes, little girl, you really do. Take the bus. Look after your brother."

Little brother takes up the theme. He's thought of another objection: he's afraid.

"Afraid of what?"

"There are wolves in the woods."

"They'll eat us all up," big sister adds.

"Stop scaring your brother," stepmother says, then turns to little brother.

"There's nothing to be afraid of," she says, kneeling down to his level, taking hold of his shoulders. "You've got to be brave. Granny will be disappointed if you don't come."

He lowers his eyes. He wants to be a good boy, doesn't want to anger Mummy, but he's still afraid.

"I will," he says in a small voice.

"Don't forget your coats," stepmother calls from the door. "It's cold out there."

Red for the girl, blue for the boy.

Little brother and big sister tell stories on the bus, striving to outdo one another with each new tale as they name the terrible monsters that live in the woods.

Shaggy, deformed things, lusting for something—anything, they creep up to houses in the middle of the night. They'll snatch a child from an open window if they get the chance. Didn't you hear about what happened to the Peterson boy?

"I don't believe you."

Big sister shrugs, looks out the window at the verge, swamped with snow.

"Believe what you like, little brother, we're nearly there."

She presses the button. The bus comes to a stop, then pulls away, leaving the two of them at the side of the road. Over there, the forest starts. They hesitate, look in both directions before crossing. There's no traffic; few people come this way.

In the forest.

"Do you want me to tell you another story?"

"No."

"Did you hear about the old houses that walk on chicken legs in the middle of the night? Witches live in them. If they catch little children out in the woods…"

"Stop it, I don't want to hear any more." He puts his hands over his ears.

"It's just a fairy story, a baby story. You don't believe in things like that, do you?"

"Of course not."

"It's the cold you have to worry about anyway. Your fingers go numb. Watch that you don't catch them on the briars. The cuts won't hurt until much later."

Out here you understand what cold is, understand that it can kill.

Deeper and deeper. No longer in sight of the road.

There's something wrong with the trees here. The feeling is there before the understanding.

Big sister is first to see. "Look."

There, high up in the bare canopy: something swings from a branch. They squint, trying to work out what it is, trying to make sense of it.

As they get closer, it resolves itself into a boy, hanging limply from a branch, wires wrapped around his neck.

"Is he dead?"

"Don't look," she says as he sways in the wind, this way, that way.

At their approach, his head snaps up, revealing a painted face, lacquered and shiny, like scrubbed pink flesh. Rose-red splodges on each cheek, long horsehair eyelashes fluttering in the breeze. Wooden limbs clack together as he struggles with the wires, spinning himself round to get a better view.

"Help me," he says in a scritchy voice, the sound of wind rustling twigs.

"What happened?" big sister calls.

"Some bad boys put me up here and I can't get down. Please, I'm all tangled up."

"Something strange is happening to your face," little brother says.

He's right: wood shouldn't be able to move like that. Something twists, something distorts. The wooden boy's arms windmill, spinning him tighter. Even so, he gets a hand up to his face, covers it.

"Christ," he shouts, "you tell one lie and they string you up for it." Then he chuckles to himself. "Get it?" he says. "String you up." Then, angry: "Tell me you've never done it."

"You're making my brother afraid," big sister says, but the marionette pays no attention.

"I can hear the trees whispering," he says in a low voice, agitated, dancing on his strings. "They're telling me what they're going to do to me."

"I think we'd better be going," big sister says, taking little brother's hand.

"Don't leave me here with them. If you do, you're as good as doing it yourselves."

They hesitate, and he becomes conciliatory.

"I knew you weren't going to leave me. Help me down. My father will reward you well. He's a rich man, a carpenter."

Little brother takes a couple of steps toward the tree, but big sister stops him.

"Liar," she says.

The marionette spins, agitated, turning upside down. "I won't hurt you. I don't mean you any harm."

Again, distortion. Something that lives beneath the surface trying to break free. Dissimulation can only get you so far. It leers, it snarls, it spits, an old spider dancing on its web.

They run, unbewitched.

His screams can be heard for a long time afterwards, high, affected. Then silence. They stop to listen, appalled. But worse is to come.

He starts chuckling again and this time he does not stop.

Will the path ever end?

It takes them deep into the woods. Big sister and little brother are afraid, though they say nothing to each other. She is older, she must look out for little brother; he is a man, he cannot show weakness. They walk close together, the only acknowledgement of their unspoken fear.

"Do you think it's far?" he asks, peering around.

These are short days and dusk will come soon. They do not want to be caught out here in the gloaming, when bravery may give way entirely.

"No," she says uncertainly. "No, not far. Don't you remember when we came in the summer and all of this was flowers and bird song?"

There are no birds singing now, only the wind through the bare branches. The muffled sounds of movement in the snow, of little falls. The screech of an owl out hunting, the triumph of a successful hunt, the rage at being thwarted.

"We came here?" little brother asks.

"With mother. We picnicked by that tree."

She points to an ancient oak, twisted and broken, the head of a flint axe embedded in its trunk, the wound almost healed over. Everything is inimical to life out here, to their kind of life: it is not wanted in this pristine landscape, unspoiled by humanity.

"It can't be far now," she says, drawing her coat round her,

They both want to go home, but neither wants to pass by the marionette again.

They have not discussed what would be worse: to see him still tangled up, still cursing, or for the branch to be bare, the wood silent.

They press on.

The snow is rabid white. They shiver together.

All quiet, all still.

Around them, faces watch from the trees: simulacra and old spirits, forced together, driven out of town and city, out of dingle and dell, pushed out into the deep wood, cleaving together, murderous and resentful.

"How far to Granny's house?" little brother asks.

"Not far."

"There are bad things out here."

"Keep going, we'll be safe. They don't attack people."

He wishes big sister's red coat wasn't so visible.

They trudge on.

Movement on the path up ahead. A boy with his dog. Massive, like a wolf, growling as they approach.

"She won't hurt you," the boy says. "She's just hungry." He looks hopefully at the hamper. "What have you got in there, food?"

They shake their heads, say: "It's all for Granny."

"She won't mind," he says. "She owes me." He turns to the dog. "We're hungry, aren't we, girl?"

"I'm sorry," big sister says, "we would if we could."

The boy looks from one to the other; his gaze settles on little brother. "You'll share it with us, won't you?"

Little brother stares back. He stoops, picks up a branch. "Don't come any closer," he says.

The other boy laughs and his dog barks.

"I mean it."

The dog comes forward. One step. Two. Little brother swings his branch through the air; the dog snarls, snaps at it.

A second pass. Little brother is carried off balance by the momentum and the dog takes its chance: leaps, jaws fixing onto his sleeve.

They're on the ground now, rolling in the snow. Little brother tries to shrug off the coat. There's a tearing sound and the sleeve comes away. The dog drops it, readies itself again; the boy is laughing.

"Give us some cake," he's shouting.

Big sister picks up the branch, brings it down hard. The boy realises the danger too late, calls to his animal: "Watch out!"

A crunch, a howl. The dog slinks back to its master, whining.

"We're going now," big sister says, helping her brother to his feet. "Don't follow us."

They back away, watching as the boy cradles the dog's head in his lap, listening to its broken whines.

"We're hungry too," he shouts after them. "Think on that when you're enjoying your cake with Granny."

But he makes no move to follow, just sits there in the red snow, stroking the dog's head and whispering to her, tears rolling down his cheeks.

There is a hut up ahead. A woodcutter's hut.

Little brother's coat hangs ragged. He keeps looking over his shoulder, imagining he can hear the dog barking still, imagining he can hear the marionette's laughter.

Blue is the colour of cold, red of heat.

He doesn't want to go anywhere near the hut; he wants to circle round it, but that way lies the deep wood.

He's shivering.

"We need to warm up," big sister says.

"Won't we be there soon?"

"Yes, soon," she says. "But you need to warm up."

He lets himself be led.

She raises the branch, pushes the door open. "Hello?" she calls, but there's no one inside. The woodcutter hasn't been out here since the snows came.

She tries to get the stove lit. The wood is wet, won't catch. She looks around for something else to keep little brother warm. Here on the floor: a skin to wrap him in, a wolf skin.

It itches.

It smells.

Gradually, he stops shivering. "Can't we stay here?" His stomach rumbles. He looks longingly at the basket.

"Granny is waiting."

Here is an axe.

"Take it," she says. "We might need it."

Little brother holds the axe, big sister the branch. He is still wrapped in his wolf skin.

They look at the trees, at the undergrowth; it is already too dark to see what might lurk in them. Ambushes come in many forms.

"Listen," she says, "the beasts are out."

"What are they?"

Not wolves, certainly. Not bears. No animal they have ever heard. Something else altogether.

"They are hunting," she says.

"Hunting for what?"

"We will be quite safe. You have your axe; I have my branch."

"Of course," he says, peering around again doubtfully.

"Look, a fire."

They approach cautiously. A clearing. Two figures, a boy and a girl, piteous in rags, trying to warm themselves at the fire. Embers smoulder, giving no heat, no relief.

They make no move to rouse themselves as big sister and little brother approach.

"We've seen you before, Mr. Wolf," they say to little brother.

"The woodcutter cut you down dead."

"Are you going to eat us, Mr. Wolf?"

"I'm not a wolf," he says.

"That's what all the wolves in boy's clothing say."

The girl shivers violently.

"Please help us. We've got food. We'll share it with you. Come, warm yourself by the fire."

And the fire burns brightly, as if at her command, but coldly too. Blue flames.

Little brother looks longingly at it.

"We must be going," big sister says.

"Stay with us," the boy says.

"Just a little while," the girl adds, patting the ground beside her. "We can protect you."

"We're going to see Granny," little brother says. "We'll be safe there."

"That's what we thought," the boy says, rubbing his hands together. "We got lost in the woods. The witch promised us sweet treats."

"Can you take us with you?" the girl asks. "Show us the way. We won't be any trouble."

"No," big sister says. "No, I don't think so."

"Give us a bit of your heat, then."

"Just a little."

"We don't need much."

"We've got nothing to give you," big sister says.

"Then we won't tell you what lies ahead."

"We don't need your help."

They back away and the children do nothing to follow. Lights dance in the motes of the fire, will-o'-the-wisps at play.

"Give us your skin to keep us warm, at least," the girl calls. "That's not too much to ask, is it, Mr. Wolf?"

They are relieved when they see the house up ahead. They almost missed it, though the trail leads straight to its door.

The house gapes, shrouded in darkness.

They call out, ring the bell. No answer.

Inside, they set down the hamper, lock the door behind them.

"Granny, Granny—it's us. Where are you, Granny?"

The hearth is bone-cold and smut-black. Granny is house-proud. She would not leave the ashes unswept in the fireplace.

"Granny doesn't believe in heating," big sister says, the words sounding thin even to her. "She's careful with her money."

The house is cold, yes, but not just cold. Empty.

A pot hangs over the dead fire. Big sister lifts the lid, peers in.

"What is it?" little brother asks.

"Don't look," big sister says.

High laughter, a dog's howl, cold light. A bowl of sweets for little children.

There is food on the kitchen counter. A ham, some bread. Nothing else. The bread is stale; the ham has a fur, as though trying to grow its bristles back, as though trying to keep warm in this terrible weather.

Little brother's stomach rumbles.

"Eat a cake," big sister says, opening the basket. "Granny won't mind now."

He manages no more than a bite. They've turned to cinders.

They try the phone, but the line's dead.

Something prowls around outside. They hear its claws scrabbling on the front door and are glad they locked it behind them.

Little brother starts shivering again. "I don't feel so good."

In the bathroom, they check the medicine cabinet. Bottles on every shelf, long out of date. Nothing for a temperature.

"Pull the skin around you, more tightly."

"It stinks," he complains.

"It will keep you warm."

"Where's Granny?"

"She hasn't heard us, that's all. She'll be in bed. We should go upstairs. We'll be safe there."

Upstairs, then. Up to Granny's bedroom, with its smell of lavender and talc.

They call out her name. The stairs creak. No one answers.

Granny's not here. They were tricked. Led into the deep dark woods. Led up the garden path.

The curtains are drawn in Granny's room. It's hard to see anything in here. Branches scratch against the glass.

"What's that in Granny's bed?"

Come closer. Grip the axe handle tightly.

"Who's that coming up the stairs?"

Little brother can't see properly. The skin slips down over his face.

The thing in the bed moves; it groans.

He can hear it now, here within his skin. It can pass through locked doors. They will never be safe.

The flash of a red coat. Something growls. Is it him?

"Take the axe," he says. "It's too heavy."

He wants to lie down, very tired. His teeth are chattering monstrously.

It's moving, sitting up.

"Kill it! Kill it!"

Little brother swings his axe.

And out in the woods the wolves are howling. And there are worse things in the woods than wolves.

And somewhere a baby is crying.

DEATHFLOWER

OLUWATOMIWA AJEIGBE

AMARA BOUGHT the potted plant from the new florist at the junction of her street. She didn't know exactly when the florist moved to her street but she had lost touch with reality for weeks after the accident, so that was understandable. She took the plant home, deciding to see it as a sign of a new beginning, as a sign of her moving on. After all, she was just following her therapist's instructions.

"Do something that makes you happy. Buy yourself a gift. Try to do things that do not remind you too much of him," he had said, peering at her through his owlish glasses.

On her way home after that day's session, she had seen the florist's shop at the junction. The big sign in front of the shop said: ***Persephone's Petals, Providing Peace In Potted Plants.*** Amara had winced at the forced alliterations but after only a second of hesitation, she walked in. Immediately, an old woman appeared and asked her what she wanted. The woman looked like she was around eighty but moved with surprising speed, beckoning to Amara to inspect the rows of potted plants and make her choice.

There were different plants in the woman's shop. Amara recognized them because before Femi died, the house had been filled with beautiful plants and flowers. She recognized sunflowers, tulips, lilies, marigolds, hyacinths, and the ubiquitous roses. The roses were everywhere and were of different colours: red, white, yellow, blue. Seeing the flowers, and especially those roses, reminded her of an evening she had spent with Femi a couple of days before the accident.

They had been on a dinner date, as was their weekly tradition. The restaurant they had chosen that night was named Rose Banquet. While she was going through the menu, Amara asked Femi a question.

"So I have actually wanted to ask this for a while," she started, "but what is the big deal with roses? They are so... overrated."

Femi had chuckled and leaned back in his chair. He was dressed in a purple-lined shirt she had picked for him while they had been shopping earlier that week. On his middle finger, his wedding band twinkled.

"Well, roses are special flowers," he said.

"Why are they so special?" Amara asked, crossing her arms.

"Well, they are very beautiful flowers. That is undeniable."

Amara made a dissenting sound but did not interrupt.

"Also, in most beliefs, roses are believed to be made by the gods. The Greeks, for example, believe that the first rose was made through the combined efforts of Chloris, Aphrodite, Dionysus, Zephyrus, and Apollo. Five gods came together to create one flower, Amarachi. Think about that. In fact, I think roses aren't rated enough."

He had adopted his professor face, the one he used to lecture his students at the university. He gestured excitedly. His eyes were faraway and shined with passion as he spoke. At a point, Amara didn't really catch his words anymore. She was lost in his beautiful brown eyes—

The old woman had to tap her lightly before she realized that she had frozen in place. She blinked and looked away from the roses. No. She would definitely not buy roses.

"I haven't seen any one I like. I think I'll just leave," she said.

The old woman clucked her tongue and shook her head.

"No. Wait here," she ordered before turning around and walking to the back of the room. Puzzled by the woman's words, Amara obeyed and stood still till she saw the woman shuffling back with a plant in her hands. When she came close enough and Amara saw the plant, she gasped.

It was the most beautiful thing she had ever seen. It bore a distinct resemblance to a rose and that almost put her off, but its beauty had caught her attention and held it. Its petals each seemed to have a different colour—red, blue, yellow, white, purple. Along its stalk, like a rose, little thorns sprouted. The plant was unlike anything she had ever seen and for the second time since she entered the florist's shop, she froze. And again, the old woman snapped her out of it.

"What about this one?" she asked, her beady eyes fixed on Amara's mesmerized face.

"I... it is so beautiful. Are you sure you want to sell it?"

"Of course, I want to sell it," the old woman retorted. "If I don't sell them, they will just die of hunger."

Amara didn't ask the old woman what she meant with her strange choice of words. The plant was the only thing she could see.

"How much is it?" she asked.

"Five thousand naira."

Amara couldn't believe her luck. Five thousand naira for such a beautiful plant? That was surely a bargain. She tried to peep behind the old woman to see if there were other plants like this but couldn't see any. She wondered if it was an endangered species or something. Femi would have known.

She counted five one-thousand naira notes and handed them to the old woman. The florist collected the cash and transferred the pot to Amara's hands. She handled the plant gingerly, holding it close to her chest.

"Ma? What is the name of this plant, please?" she asked the old woman. There was no answer. Amara looked up but the old woman was nowhere to be found. She called out again but was met with silence and the whispering of hundreds of plants.

She turned and walked out of Persephone's Petals, clutching her plant to her chest like a lifeline, like a potted piece of her lost peace.

Every night, Amara tried to sleep. And every night, she failed.

The dreams that disrupted her sleep always start with Femi saying goodbye. Every night, she relived the day she lost him forever. She remembered inhaling his cologne while they hugged, she remembered the softness of his lips as he kissed her goodbye, she remembered him promising to return before dark, she remembered the phone call from a stranger later that evening, breaking the terrible news to her.

The house started feeling empty without him, too quiet without his booming laughter. In her dreams, the silence smothered her till she couldn't breathe anymore, till her lungs got filled with the emptiness, till everything became still.

The plant's presence comforted her. She placed it on her bedside table and admired its otherworldly beauty. Sometimes, when she was startled awake by another nightmare, she reached out and touched the petals of the plant. Once, she thought she heard a sigh of pleasure coming from the plant as she ran her hand over its petals but the thought passed as she slipped back into sleep.

A week after she bought the plant, Amara summoned enough courage to go into the library. The library was the largest room in the house. Ceiling to floor bookshelves stood on every side of the room. Amara knew that the books were arranged by genre and subject. Fiction took a whole shelf while the others mostly contained textbooks. Femi's botany books, all of them, stood neatly on their shelves. She ran her hands down their spines, reading the titles: *Botany, An Introduction. A Study Of Thallophytes. A Student's Guide To Kingdom Plantae.* There were several other books there. This had been Femi's favourite room in the house. Amara had not been able to cross the threshold since the funeral. She knew the reason was because she was still living in denial somehow. She knew that if she stepped into the library and Femi was not there at his desk, reading with his glasses perched on his nose, then he was truly gone. She couldn't bear to be reminded of his passing so strongly, so she avoided the library. But she had to go in if she wanted to know what type of plant she had bought.

She searched for a long time. There were books that seemed to be encyclopaedias of all the plants in the world, with diagrams beside them. But none of them was her mysterious plant. After wasting several hours in the library, she gave up.

When she returned to her bedroom, she looked down at the plant. It didn't seem to have a name or maybe she just didn't know where to look. She knew it couldn't be poisonous though. It had been in the house for days and she had touched it several times without rashes appearing on her skin or anything like that. Amara stared at its colourful petals and slender body. Its small leaves seemed to be waving at her as she watched.

"Aphrodite," she said.

The name sounded fitting. The Greek goddess of beauty. Somehow, she knew the plant liked the name. When she went to bed that night, for the first time in weeks, she fell into a dreamless sleep.

The morning after Amara named the plant, it took her blood.

She had been watering it, cupping her hand in a bowl and sprinkling the water on Aphrodite when she felt a light sting. Her hand had brushed against one of Aphrodite's thorns and blood welled from the cut. She watched, transfixed, as the blood dropped on the plant.

It shivered visibly, shaking, then suddenly it started growing before her eyes till it was as tall as her. Amara stepped backwards as fast as she could, putting enough distance between her and the growing plant. She watched as it leaned ever so slightly in her direction, its petals convulsing.

She shook her head, thinking she was seeing things or that she was in a dream.

This is not a dream.

The voice was a sibilant whisper in her mind and it startled her so much that she tripped and fell to the floor. As she struggled to a sitting position and scuttled backwards from the plant, she heard herself saying one word over and over.

"No no no no no no no..." She chanted, as if the word had the power to change the reality in which she had so suddenly found herself.

Yes, Amarachi. Your blood has awakened me. Now, I shall feast in earnest.

Amara did not wait to hear what else the plant had to say. She stumbled out of the door, running out of the house as fast as she could. It was raining outside. She didn't care. She plunged into the rain, not minding that she was barefooted or that she was still dressed in her pyjamas. She ran as fast as she could on the uneven road, raindrops pelting her body and stinging her face.

She stopped at the junction of her street and looked to her left. A barbershop, a supermarket, and between them...nothing. She blinked. There was no sign of Persephone's Petals. She wiped the raindrops from her face and peered closer at the shops lining both sides of the street. The florist's shop remained unseen.

"Looking for me?"

Amara turned around so fast that she lost her balance and fell for the second time that morning but into a puddle this time. Standing over her, a black umbrella over her head, was the florist. The old woman appeared the same as before but this time she was dressed in black rags. The holes in her ragged gown let Amara see through to her flesh. Her skin was a chalky grey and when the old woman stooped and touched Amara's face, it felt like she was being touched by a tree.

"You silly child," the old woman said, tracing a finger down Amara's jaw line. "Are you ready to join your husband in the afterlife?"

Amara couldn't move or speak. She just stared into the woman's eyes. Her eyes were a startling green and seemed to see deep into Amara's mind. Those eyes saw her deepest secrets. Amara knew then that nothing could be hidden from those eyes.

"I can see the answer in your soul. It is not one that pleases me," the old woman said, rising to her full height.

"I will leave you to suffer a little bit more."

There was a flash of lightning and for a split second an aged tree with grey bark and bloodred leaves stood in the woman's place.

Then the darkness moved in and Amara fell into it.

Amara woke up in her bed, in her room, gasping.

For a second, she was disoriented. In her mind's eye, she was looking up at an ancient tree with bleeding leaves while the rain lashed at her skin. Then she blinked the vision away and looked around. She was in her room alright.

She looked at her bedside, expecting to find the monstrous plant that had wanted to devour her. But she saw Aphrodite as its normal self. She looked down at her body. She was not wet or dirty from running and falling in the rain. Outside, she could hear the patter of raindrops still hitting the roof.

Had it all been a dream? She wondered.

Amara looked at the plant again. Something did not feel right. She felt like she was the butt of a very twisted joke. Even though the plant looked like her regular Aphrodite, the potted plant with exotic flowers she had bought from the old florist, she had a feeling something was amiss. She was certain that she did not want to spend her nights with the plant by her side, especially after what had happened.

She got out of bed and got a mop from the corner of the room. Using the mop's long handle, she pulled and pushed the clay pot until the plant was out of the room. She kept pushing it from a distance, still too unnerved to touch it herself, until she managed to push it into the first room she could find. It was the library. She threw in the mop after it, as if it had now become tainted by whatever evil force dwelled in the plant, before shutting the door.

Amara planned to try looking for the florist again. She wasn't sure if her experience that morning had been a dream or vision or some sort of reality but she had a lot of questions about the plant and about the florist herself.

The hard rain didn't stop falling throughout the day though.

Amara had to give up on looking for the florist and decided to take the plant out first thing the next morning.

That night, she dreamt about Femi.

He was walking towards her on a forest path. He was dressed in the clothes he'd been wearing the last time she saw him alive; a black jacket, a blue shirt, and black jean trousers. She called out to him and walked towards him too, filled with happiness that she was seeing him again.

But as he got closer, she realized that something was wrong. Femi's skin was greyish, as if all the blood and colour had been drained from him. His eyes leaked a reddish liquid, as if he was weeping. When she looked down at his feet, instead of the sneakers he had been wearing on the day of the accident, he had roots as legs. The roots made it difficult for him to walk properly so he had to drag himself towards her.

Amara backpedalled, appalled by the sylvan horror that looked like her husband. Femi kept coming closer and somehow Amara knew that even if she suddenly sprouted wings and flew away, he would still find her. She kept moving backwards till she had her back against a tree. Femi got closer and closer. His grey face split in a grin as he approached. Amara turned to look at the tree to see if she could climb it, maybe she could buy herself more time. But when she looked up, she gasped.

The tree was the same one she had seen after her encounter with the old woman in the rain. Its leaves were a vivid red but not the red of leaves in autumn. The leaves did not fall. The tree's bark was grey, like ash. Amara touched it and was surprised by how smooth it was. It felt... it felt like skin.

A hand touched her shoulder and she jumped. She had forgotten about Femi. He was so close to her now that she could not run if she wanted to. His arms were spread wide, as if he was expecting her to hug him. She didn't want to but there was nothing she could do about it.

When she looked down at her feet, she saw that Femi's leg roots had joined with the roots of the tree with red leaves, holding her in place. Femi hugged her and she felt something shift inside her. She was slowly being absorbed into him. She could see her skin losing its colour till it attained an ashy shade. She wanted to scream but her tongue was glued to the roof of her mouth. She knew, somehow, that she was turning into a tree like Femi.

In her head, she could hear the old florist's voice as she laughed. It was the cold laughter that uprooted her from the dream back to her room, drenched in sweat with a scream trapped in her throat.

Immediately she opened her eyes, Amara knew something was very, very wrong.

She laid in bed, staring up at the spinning ceiling fan. The dream stayed with her, haunting her mind like a vile ghost. She could still feel the pain of her bones being liquefied and reshaped till they became wood. She could still feel her legs getting entwined in Femi's roots till she couldn't move anymore.

She blinked. Femi's face stayed with her too. The way sap had been leaking from his eyes, the way he moved like an automaton, that crazy grin, the greyness of his dead skin...

Amara closed her eyes and shook her head to dispel the image.

Do not try to forget.

She sat up straight, suddenly wide awake. The voice that had spoken in her head was the same sibilant whisper that had come from Aphrodite after she had cut her finger on its thorns. But the plant couldn't be talking to her. It was faraway in the library. It was impossible.

"W-who... what are you?" she stammered, wondering if she was going crazy.

My identity is of no use to you, since you'll be dead soon. But if you must know, I am called Ewe-Iku, *the flower of death.*

Amara had lost track after the way the voice had mentioned her dying so flippantly. She wondered if she could run out of the house before the plant could grow into a monstrous form and kill her but again. It plucked the thought from her mind.

You cannot run. Rise. Go to your window.

Trembling, she obeyed. She slid out of bed. The air from the fan chilled her now that she wasn't under the covers. She walked to the window, where she could see the front gate and looked.

The death flower was right, she saw at once. The massive black gate that led in or out of the house was covered by crawling vines. Amara was certain that Femi had never had any type of ivy in the compound. He had always said he would only have those type of creeping plants when they got a bigger house, preferably in the countryside.

The vines on the gate were deep red and seemed to be mobile. Even as Amara watched, they slithered like snakes and covered every inch of the gate. There was no way she could leave the compound. She turned away from the window.

As you can see, I brought some friends.

"Why me? Why is this happening to me?" Amara's voice cracked. She held her head in her hands, wishing the whole nightmare would stop. For a couple of seconds, there was silence and she allowed herself to think that the voice was gone or had been a figment of her imagination. Then the door to her room was torn off its hinges and the death flower formerly known as Aphrodite walked into the room.

At least, to the stunned Amara, it seemed to be walking. It was much taller than her now. Its flowers were like little heads all turned towards her. In their midst, she could see several sharp teeth. The plant had outgrown its pot and was moving around on its roots, much like Femi had been in her dream.

Amara's mouth worked but no sound came forth.

Why you? Because you were unlucky to marry from the family of people dedicated to the great spirit of the blood tree. You married a child of the forest and when a child of the forest dies, their partner must die too.

Amara wanted to protest, to say that it was unfair. But all the strength had been sapped out of her. She just knelt there, looking up at the plant. She realized then that the old woman must be the spirit of the blood tree. Everything started to make sense—why Femi had loved plants so much, why she had seen the florist shop after the funeral, why the old woman asked if she was ready to join Femi in the afterlife.

But it was too late. She couldn't move. She was rooted in place and could only watch as the death flower descended and lowered its many teeth to devour her.

HUSTERIA

CHARLOTTE TURNBULL

IT WAS LATE when the French man pushed the black bars of the gates, driving them deep into the moat of snow sheathing the house and covering the gardens. I watched him from the study window, dancing a misted tumbler from hand to hand. The driveway was a long, white tongue but eventually he tripped on the boot-scraper and fell to his knees between the pillars. I do not like company. As my father once sneered, before the old ratfink died of greed. "You have been cursed, Emma, with self-sufficiency"—his favourite thing about me, that I asked nothing of him.

Remy had been drinking in the village when the snow fell untimely, as it can in April. We had slept together occasionally; always at his, never at mine, but not enough for his liking or so he had said when calling it off, telling me he liked to be loved. He had been on his way home when he heard fell cries in the squall.

"Wild things are out there," Remy shivered in the drawing room drying his coat on an ottoman in front of the fireplace. I tucked a stray hair back into my tight bun and ran the brocade of my dressing gown through my fingers, trying to remember when I had last been in this room, the dust in stiff sculptures.

"You shouldn't be alone tonight," he said urgently. His curly brown hair flattened as fluffs of snow melted to heavy water, his eyes shining beads in the firelight.

I crossed my arms. "How much have you had to drink?"

An ancient game of Solitaire stretched across the felted card table. He shuffled the cards in a one-hand cascade with a grin. "Poker?" he asked. My laughter echoed, weaving behind statues in the alcoves, trailing over the portraits up the stairs. It stopped me from saying 'No,' the word thickening in my gullet until I nearly choked. "It'll be fun," he added, having to explain.

It wasn't especially, and how I managed to lose with this poker-face —but regardless. He took his coat, seeing me unthawed to the last, but at the front door, the blizzard drove. His eyes darted left and right, fearful of the howling. I was not yet a monster, so I offered him supper.

I tugged cobwebs from chandeliers, replacing a bulb or two, and took a damp cloth to the long dining table, setting two places with tarnished silver. I boiled pasta and buttered bread. The wine was nutty and brown, but he charged his glass to me anyway, the fool.

He asked, *"faire le tour de chateau."* There was no light, and I couldn't find the correct fuse box. So by the glow of a candelabra, I pulled back the bed curtains to show him where he could sleep.

"Why is there a—a—*cercueil* in here?" Remy unbuttoned his shirt in front of a long wooden chest buried in the corner beneath unworn clothes and unread books.

"It's not a coffin. It's a family heirloom." I remembered lying in it as a child, stretching fingers and toes to reach either end so I might know how it felt to be a woman.

He threw the shirt over one end of the chest where a tiny portion of carved roses and brambles were exposed, and undid his trousers.

"Are you a vampire?" He pulled me to him, kissing me hopefully. He offered to do many things; some generous, some selfish. There was a relic of arousal, but I always was repelled by vulnerability; his need to be laughed at one moment, taken seriously the next.

"You're not like the others, with their claws and tears," he said, dissolving into a rustle of sheets, slither of eiderdown, and an imperfect grasp of English.

He was still propositioning me as I took the stairs to my room in the eaves.

Under a knot of low beams, I lay on my narrow cot when a shriek in the woods beyond the gardens drew me to the small window. I wiped condensation from the pane. There were flashes between the trees; the moon glancing at something silky and lustrous. It vaulted up into the white veil; leaving behind nothing but two huge black paw-prints, which quickly filled with snow.

Its chaotic presence put me in mind of something I hadn't thought of in so long. Leaning over the side of the bed I saw it; the small, dusty-white plastic box, lid pierced with air holes. I shook the box gently, wondering if it was still in there, wondering why, if I resisted relationships, I still kept it like this? I thought of the animals outside, but I wasn't like them; claws and tears.

Lifting up one end of the lid, carefully, I tipped the box into the light. I smiled, spread my legs, and let it crawl back inside.

The moon was a plump handful as I stood naked in it, peeling back the bed-curtains to watch him sleep. His legs reached so far that feet emerged into frosted air either side of the broad mattress.

It was a frenzied and piggish night of little sleep.

Next morning at the front door, he held my hand delicately like it was a fragile animal. I had the unnerving sense of completing a necessary narrative; a brief reprieve from a constant melancholy feeling of missing an organ—a lung, or a kidney.

"*Je t'aime,*" he said.

But I wasn't listening; wondering only whether there was time to push him to the floor? To rally our cries for one final brief thunder? I checked my watch, there wasn't. I longed for him. And he bored me.

I patted his arm. He dropped my hand like he'd been bitten, but I had gone before he'd even left the door step.

Snow had melted as fast as it had fallen. Lawns gleamed viscid and sodden slick. Spring had hatched overnight, and everywhere green shoots poked through the soil.

I whipped back curtains, throwing up windows in every room forgetting why there was such decay. Merry breezes kicked dust into corners and custard beams of sunlight transformed abandon into treasure.

I span the gold taps in the many-mirrored bathroom, and sank into the bath surrounded by a multitude of beautiful goddesses; tresses messed and perfect; rosy skin steaming from ichor; eyes green as pine; and brows thick with intellect.

I turned to see where the light was coming from, to better understand my new illumination, and noticed the empty plastic box on the sink. Inside me, it plucked my strings until I thrummed like a harp.

When I left the bathroom, I dropped the box into the bin.

Through a window I saw my beloved roses had curled back verdant jackets to show a glimpse of the coy pink petal within.

Commonly, I prefer to do everything in writing. Precise, detailed notes —implicating paper trails that nobody can neglect or overlook. So the board was surprised to hear me join a conference call, but I was a delight—I may even have made a joke.

In the past I felt self-conscious about taking my father's place on the board, despite the fact that I have a double-first, and did every menial little job it was possible to do at the company first. When the miserable bastard died I insisted that they interview internally and externally before accepting the role.

Today I realised I was an excellent Chairman and tousled my hair, even though nobody could see me. I couldn't stop giggling.

But late that night at my desk, I struggled with a strategy document, hitting a panicked loop of thought about how Remy had not called. He was a prince to haunt dreams, wasn't he? How I had begged him to stay for supper! I might as well have pinned him down.

I sifted through applications for a new role, gnawing at a nail to realise everyone was more qualified than me. The nail came away in my teeth. I tapped the dry, flaking bed left behind, and another nail slipped straight out. One by one they pulled away, with nothing to cling to. I ran to the kitchen, collected them into a tea cup, blaming poor self-care, trying to contain myself. On the kitchen floor was a trail of gilded hairs.

I limped the floors of that poorly heated, ill-lit house, bought to diversify my investments. I had allowed my father to furnish it, and it showed. I tiptoed through, trying not to make an impact, following the hair loss, gathering it on a plate, crawling after each fine piece of myself—to leave none behind.

The plate of hair was on the dining table, next to the tea cup of nails, and as my dry tongue tried to swallow the nightmare, a tooth came loose. One by one I dropped them into a soup bowl, running tongue around empty, parched gums.

I could have cried, privately, where nobody would see and misconstrue it, but my ducts were now empty.

The bathroom was an infinity of bald, toothless crones. Eyelashes fell like pine needles with each slow blink. My belly was taut, prickable as a balloon. A pain wrapped itself around my torso so tightly that it pushed the air out of me. I reached back to the spine straining against skin. Between breaths I grasped about for some explanation or clue. Pressure built, drawing everything down. I eased into the bath, and clung to the rolling sides.

—and then blood rushed through my ears. I wept scarlet runnels, and there was explosion between my legs. I heaved viscous, sticky red vomit and couldn't understand why I was not yet dead.

The flow lightened, but the pain matured. The mirrors made the room an abattoir. I pulled the plug, coughing up tiny black balls of sputum. The bright blood now drained into a dark molass at the plughole. I showered until the water ran pink. Wrapped in towels, I reached for painkillers.

Curled on my cot, erratic gushes and spurts quickly soaked the bedding so I lined the bath with old towels to sleep fitfully, too scared to move, jaw throbbing, itching and burning all over.

During the night doors slammed from winds billowing through the open windows. The house seemed angrily disapproving.

I woke sweating to hot dawn breaking through the window. Coarse, dark, oily hair clumped over everything; legs, torso, breasts, arms. I recoiled from my own leathery, sausage fingers and fell from the bath with unexpected low gravity. In the many mirrors, I was surrounded by an army of beasts. They dug at themselves with scimitar claws. Feeling the gouges, I realised the claws were mine.

I grasped a razor but the hair grew back as I watched.

The emergency services said it was not an emergency. The GP reassured me there were options available and advised me to come in for a chat.

"But—I'm a monster," I whispered. "What will people think?"

"It's up to you," he said.

I sent a message to the board apologising for myself. *I'm probably making a fuss about nothing,* I wrote—relaxed, easy-going—and then went back to bed. The garret stairs were too slight for my new heft so I slipped between Remy's dirty sheets, exhausted but fretful, unable to sleep.

In the late afternoon steam rose from my pelt in the heat. The walls seemed to be on fire but I shut windows and closed curtains. Greasy darkness churned inside. The fruit bowl made me so angry that I threw it, bowl and all, through the curtains and window, to shatter on the garden path below. I mixed a cake of sugar and salt and ate it raw, swallowing lumps. I ate and ate, but the emptiness inside dilated.

In the bathroom mirrors, I was brutishly everywhere; squaring wide shoulders; shaking manes; thrusting barreled chests. The leering pitchfork of tusks. This patchwork of nature, of power and beauty, when so combined, seemed perversely man-made; what part of me could be hidden in there?

But my memories were intact. This other, was also me.

Cans of soup crushed and glugged like baby's milk, one after another, dribbled into my ruff. Reduced to a pulsing greed, shamed by the need to be brimful and bursting, I went hunting.

Scarf around my face, hood pulled low, sweat slicked my fur together.

In the village shop I had a coughing fit and hacked up a ball of sticky hair. The congealing blood stank. I spat it into my scarf, and the owner leaned over the counter.

"If you come in here in this state again, I will call the police."

Some teenage girls passed me, mooching along the lane, silken bellies reflecting the golden afternoon. Saliva glooped from the jaw jutting from the scarf. I licked my lips. The girls nudged and laughed. I roared, thundering fat fists against bowled chest.

A mother with a pram scissored in and out, nervously overtaking. I saw myself briefly reflected in a newborn's black eyes. Mouth gaping, no vestige of humanity left, I imagined swallowing the infant neat to fill the hole. It was a fearful primal hunger.

I was suddenly desperate to be hidden at home.

But a small dog was tied to a post outside the greengrocers. I snatched it and ran.

Inside the house, the poor dog shivered in my arms.

I snapped its neck before sinking it deep.

Resting on my haunches, I opened my laptop, thick, taloned digits smacking at the keyboard. The phone rang. My dead father's business partner left a message suggesting I take a break to consider whether I was in the right role.

I deleted the message and lay supine on the floor drinking an old bottle of cooking brandy and eating fleas picked from the fur of my own belly.

I checked my emails. *Lock your doors*—Remy had sent a link to a local paper. The shadowy photo was me—*beasts on the loose*.

I wanted him. I wanted to kill him.

"Aidez-moi?" I purred softly through the front door, eye to the peep hole.

"I can't help you if you won't let me in," he replied, charmed, with a supermarket bag of grapes and an unripe rose torn from my own bush.

"You have to love what's on the inside," I said. "– Are you still there?"

"I can't help you if you won't let me in," he repeated, more firmly.

I unlatched the door and backed into the drawing room, huddled, reduced, obedient—forepaws between hind legs.

"What—is that? Where are you?" He called, poised for fight or flight.

I was low, in submission, claws beseeching. But he darted out across the hallway, into the dining room. I lumbered after, clambering over the dining table. Nails, teeth and hair flew from the dining service. Remy shrieked, raking bits of me from his body, shaking his clothes, as he looped around the table.

He took the stairs two at a time. I took them in fives and had him by the ankle, but he dropped his trousers and ran into the master bedroom. He was heading for the window when I tossed him onto the bed.

My leathery digit traced his collar bone, rubbed his jacket lapel with sensitive pads. I smelt them with a flattened nose, licked them, grunting when it tasted good.

Crawling backwards Remy fell off the bed, and pulled the wooden chest from its bier. I tripped over it, but finally he was cornered.

Kiss me, I whispered, pulling his ankles through my legs, my low weight over him.

But he flung his head back, screaming loud enough to make Fay Wray proud.

So I dragged him down to the cellars, his head bouncing like a ball on each step.

Remy curled up in a corner of my damp subterranean chamber. He shouted my name over and over, so I thumped and hooted. I chomped and foamed to better display my tusks. I fluffed up my mane. I displayed my power, and yet still he did not love me.

I crawled close, maw wide, knowing I contained within me the divine ability to reduce him to his composite parts and recreate him anew in perpetual variety, if only he would give me the chance.

Please, he moaned. *Please.*

I locked the door to the cellars and raged through the house pulling pictures from walls, tearing curtains from pelmets. In the kitchen I set the gas running and struck my claws against the rough flagstones, sparking the air alight.

Outside, the moon led a fugue as I vaulted across the forest.

At first, dry earth cracked under my tread, but I learned to carry the weight a little lighter; to trot on my fists. The moon led West through the night, until it set, and I picked up a familiar, reassuring scent.

In her garden, at the end of an avenue of orange trees my mother reclined in an ornamental pond, shaded by a picnic umbrella. A bright sarong knotted behind her neck, she dabbed herself with a flannel. She sat up when she saw me, water sliding from her, fine feathery fins quivering.

I hadn't seen my mother since she'd threatened me with a knife. She had insisted that she was only taking hold of it—*"to feel something splinter in my hand"* –when I had told her I was going to work for my father. I had demonised her lack of control, but I was surprised I could ever have been so disturbed by this small, translucent-looking woman.

"Emma!" I stepped straight into the pond, displacing most of the water, and into her arms. "Did you lose your key, my dear?" She sighed, like it mattered.

"How long have you had gills?" I sniffed.

"Oh, they come and go," she said, bashfully splashing water over her legs. "It's worse at night." She combed her hands through my fur even though it was greying now, and wirey. "I thought you'd decided the box was too old-fashioned."

"I had." I tapped my tusks, grim. "Loneliness isn't the only monster lurking under the bed."

"You sound like your father. He'd have us all locked up in attics," she said. "Isn't this lovely and thick, though?"

I rolled over, wretched, and she stroked my soft belly.

The house was blackened and smoky. The furnishings had gone but the fire had lost momentum within the implacable, damp walls.

I swept ash from the wooden chest and opened it, releasing a musk of ancient sweat. *It isn't as uncomfortable as it looks,* she had said. *And it's quite manageable once you're in a routine.*

I lay back into the crimson velvet lining. Manacled the trunks of my ankles. Chains ran between my legs and joined with two wide wrist cuffs. I snapped one wrist in and lifted the other paw to pull the lid down. In the dark I snapped the other cuff on against the side of the box and waited.

They are soundproofed so we can't bother anybody. I woke up a day later. The swelling had gone down; feet and hands slipped easily from the restraints. Pushing back the lid, I sat up and scratched my neck; a sticky mat of hair came away. I took the bloody flake of pelt by one corner and looked at it closely.

The hairy rind peeled off to slippery, raw skin beneath. In some places it came away quickly, dry and scabrous, in others ripping painfully. Piece by piece I flushed myself away. Afterwards, in the shower, I scrubbed a gluey substance from my skin, and washed my hair three times. Then, finally, I was done.

There were now hundreds of greasy T-zones. Was it possible to miss the great vigour of my monstrous form? To miss the change of perspective? Don't people drink and take drugs to take leave of themselves?

But standing over the dark chest, I wondered how my mother had been brave enough to make herself abhorred when there were alternatives. I pushed it back into the corner of the room, to return to the exile; no godly highs, but no monstrous lows.

Well-protected in the dank cellar, Remy was relieved to see me. He was starving and ashamed for having soiled himself during his ordeal.

Vite! he said. *It'll destroy us all!*

I want to break up, I muttered and showed him out.

In the clinic I sat exposed in a gown, feet in stirrups, nervous, although it was one of the most common procedures they did, and I'd already done it once before.

The doctor jammed his hand in and prised it out quickly. I barely felt it leave. He smirked at me as it jerked about, dangling naked, screaming in his grip.

I immediately felt different.

Vacant. Remote.

Chilled.

The doctor gave it to me in another small, white plastic box peppered with air holes, and instructions for maintenance. *Room temperature and dark. Keep air holes clear. Access to water. Avoid eye contact, but keep it healthy in case you ever decide to use it.* The doctor lent across the desk and patted my hand.

"Don't touch it, no matter how distressed it seems, or it won't learn. Don't get into this state again," he said. "It's not fair on the rest of us."

I had forgotten the sound of the sobbing.

I had put an eye to an air hole, watched it scrabble at the sides of the box, trying to gain a purchase, looking for a way out—for a way back into me. I did as I'd been told, and pushed it under the bed again.

Now, back at my desk, I could hear it; down two flights of stairs, through three closed doors, from my room.

Its cries floated through the lacuna of the house. Had it felt so wrong the first time round? How did I ever learn to sleep through it? The doctor had reassured me that a lot of us live like this. Do they also want to cradle it, kissing the tears from its face, swearing never to be parted from it again?

I went outside for a walk, to escape the thick grey atmosphere, into the clear spring air. Wrapping my mantle close I shut the front door so hard that the lion knocker slammed hard down on itself like a phantom visitor. I could still hear my Hustera screaming from its box underneath my bed in the attic.

In the garden the roses had collapsed from their premature bloom, blighted by the sudden return of cold weather. Shed pink petals lined the path, softening the sound of my footfall so it could no longer be heard.

The house stood granite firm, blindly victorious, and beyond the gates the world was flat and paper-thin like I might slowly tear it all apart and what was left would be neither here nor there.

Rempel '22

APERTURE

DAN HOWARTH

IT DOESN'T MATTER when Gemma arrives; the photographers are always there. Whether she escapes the house on a Sunday morning or Sunday afternoon, the three men wait for her in the same position every time. She knows they aren't waiting for her, but she's unable to look at them without feeling as though they expect her presence every week in the same way she anticipates them.

She walks down the promenade. A flat concrete expanse. A busy road to her left, with cars zipping too fast towards ice cream shops and cafes and the cinema. Typical seaside day-trippers. Here too briefly to appreciate the place as fully as those who live there. To her right, the sea is a molten blast of liquid steel. Livid on the edge of her vision, continuing its rapacious crawl towards the land.

Out of sight beneath the railings, children shriek and play in the sand. From Gemma's point of view, they're the wrong side of Christmas. There's still a chill to the air but the days are getting lighter and longer. The sun visits more often and so do the tourists, every person she passes on the promenade stealing a part of this town from her. The fair-weather visitors. Here for a good time but not for a long time. Does that put her in the opposite category she wonders, hands in pockets, salt on her tongue?

She doesn't remember when she first noticed the photographers, but they only appear on a Sunday. By appointment it seems. She takes this walk up and down New Brighton promenade most days. In the week, when she steps away from her two work monitors and steals some fresh air, she doesn't see them. She barely sees anyone.

She nears their usual spot. A part of the promenade that raises up, a gentle slope that rises and falls for no apparent reason. The sea wall stands tall, a full six feet, blocking the sea and the sand from those walking past. There's a step, popular with kids and a good escape for adults from the dog shit that blights this part of the town. The photographers always stand up here, sentinels over the beach. Their preferred spot is right next to one of those telescopes that you pay to use. A pound to be afforded a better view across the water to Liverpool. A glimpse of a more prosperous and metropolitan way to live, apparently.

As usual, they don't turn towards her when she walks by but that doesn't stop her feeling their eyes on her. They don't look away from their cameras and the lenses don't once turn in her direction, but there's still a pressure on the side of her face, that sense of someone watching. An inexplicable need to look up and make eye contact with the person watching.

They wear their familiar uniforms. Kagoules over the top of a brightly coloured fleece jacket. A red collar always visible on the man in the middle, garish compared to his deep green waterproof. Lightly coloured and immaculate slacks. Leather walking boots. Their cameras are identical. Black bodies and cream telephoto lenses. Their thick heads of grey hair play in the breeze. She's never once seen them wear hats or gloves in cold weather nor shorts when it gets warmer. Yet every week when she gets home and thinks of these men, she's unable to remember when she first saw them or any occasion she's seen anything of their faces beyond the glimpses visible around the cameras.

As she passes them, she stares, trying to sear the detail into her memory. She stops walking and stands behind them, hands on hips, watching them at work. They stand still, unmoving; their fingers hover over the buttons of their cameras but they don't take any pictures. She waits, trying to catch movement or the plastic *click* of the shutter closing. Nothing. Just the gulls wheeling and crying like living arrows in the sky.

Cold gnaws on her fingers and tries to worm its way beneath her jacket and jogging bottoms. Chilled air makes her lungs ache, and she pats the inhaler in her pocket, more as reassurance than out of need. She turns away from the photographers, meaning to head off down to the end of the promenade as is her usual loop. A man on a bike rings his bell, swinging round her at the last minute, so close that he displaces the air in front of her. A scent of sweat and isotonic drinks wafts across her face leaving her too shaken to vent her anger. She puts her hands on her knees, taking a breath, calming the heartbeat that chisels at her ribcage.

As she straightens up, she catches movement from the photographers. She looks round as they snap back to their original positions. The slightest echo of motion. She frowns, they're settled in their usual positions, lenses staring blankly out over the beach. Their backs to her. Their fingers poised.

She can't prove it but she's certain that as the cyclist swerved round her, she caught the reflection of the photographers' lenses in her peripheral vision. As though they'd swung round to capture her potentially being injured by the bike. Half distracted by the sound of another approaching cyclist, she looks at the backs of their heads, the thick curls of grey hair that stare back. There's no movement, no acknowledgement of her existence. Just any other Sunday.

She looks to her left, towards the end of the promenade, her usual destination. The flat concrete path doesn't hold anything for her of interest. Looking at it, she's unsure why she persists with this same route when the true thrust of the town is blocked from her view. She turns back on herself, the cyclist that nearly hit her is a weaving, luminous blob of lycra in the distance. The sound of his bell and shouted curses still rings in her ears as she finds the nearest set of concrete steps and makes her way down onto the muddy sand of the beach below.

The beach is a different world to the promenade. Brighter and quieter, away from the foreboding concrete walls and constant plod of traffic. The sand is deep brown around her feet, splattered and bunched up the walls and the steps. Down here there's a different perspective. The sea closer to the shore than it appeared from higher up, racing towards the wall, every wave trying to outdo the one before it.

Beyond the shimmering grasp of the sea stand red and white cranes. The docklands, once so proud and illustrious, now reduced to background for photographs. In front of that, way off to her right, the lighthouse. Immaculate and proud. A Victorian relic, it turns its nose up at tourists and local businesses alike. Although its purpose is extinguished, it looks in rude health, its white stones the only thing gleaming in the flat afternoon light.

Gemma walks beneath the photographers, feeling their lenses skirt over her and then pass on. She stands directly beneath them, out of their way, making it so the photographers would have to lean down, perhaps risking their necks to be able to see her. With her back to the seawall, she looks out over the sand. Straining for the detail that brings these three middle-aged men to the same spot every week without exception. They must have families at home, wives who wait for them. Perhaps visiting children and grandchildren wondering why Grandad can't make time for his photography buddies on every other day of the week.

Instead, they come here and photograph the flat beach with its dull late winter colours. Everything in shades of brown and grey and black. Nothing becomes vibrant in this town until at least March, if not later. When the colour returns to the sky and the fairground fills with children. A thought that should bring a smile sets her jaw. The time when the town stops becoming hers and is open to the world once again.

Leaning back on the wall she listens for chatter or the click of a shutter from the men above her. Wind billows her jacket and children play near the sea. But she can't hear anything from above her. Three men, just watching. Gulls flap by, spinning and chasing each other on the wind. Flying in tight formations and then breaking away, doubling back, nipping at each other as they scan the sand for scraps and detritus. Their swoops and dives draw no photos from the men above. Nor does the chug of a boat off to the right. A short, snub-nosed white schooner with barnacles and green stains.

There's a shriek from the waterfront. Her gaze drawn to the playing children. Two mothers stand on the sand, their jeans rolled up to their knees, hands held up above their eyes. A little boy tugging at one of them. The three of them pointing out to sea. Another child stumbles into view, out of the spray. Drenched and walking on flat, cold feet. The girl collapses at the feet of her mother. Her sobs out of rhythm and out of control as she heaves up and down on the ground, covered in sand and seaweed.

Before she realises what she's doing, Gemma is stood by them, her hand cupped above her eyes against the glare from the sea. It drops away. Finds her mouth. Gritty sand onto her lips and her tongue. Dirt between her teeth.

A corpse floats face down in the shallow sea. Gliding an inch over the sand. One of the women shrieks again, the sound shrill and avian like the gulls above. Scavengers that would only need the opportunity to turn this corpse into a meal. The woman's child starts to cry, hugging her legs and burying his face in her jeans. He's too young to know exactly what's wrong other than the fact his mother is upset. The other woman guides her daughter towards their crying friends and slips into the sea, not flinching at the chill.

She hauls the corpse onto the dry land, bent double with the effort. The man's face drags in the sand. His hair sodden and tangled. His skin the colour of fried mushrooms. The woman puts her fingers to the side of his neck, searching for a pulse in the ultimate display of wishful thinking. She shakes her head at her friend who whimpers in response. Both children start to cry. The woman kneeling by the corpse sees Gemma standing behind her friend and frowns at her.

"I've called 999," Gemma says. "Police and ambulance on their way. They just said to keep others away from the scene until they can get there. Shouldn't be long."

This part of the beach is deserted apart from the five of them. Further down, a pair of Golden Labradors splash in and out of the waves, chasing a ball hurled by an enormous man. The children calm down, seize up their buckets and spades and start to dig crude sand-castles, away from the shoreline.

"You go and play with them," Gemma says. "I'll deal with the emergency services when they come."

She turns her back on the corpse and watches the parents go through the motions with their kids. The two women keep looking up, turning their heads towards the corpse before looking down at the sand, ashamed of their curiosity. By the time sirens crack open the air, the children are absorbed in nothing but their game.

The police officers lead two paramedics down the stone steps, they carry a stretcher and backpacks of equipment. When they see the corpse, they stop running, the emergency nullified. Behind them, the photographers stand at the front of a growing crowd. Rubberneckers and passers-by standing and gawking. Eyes fixed on the only still body on the beach. Nobody looks at the photographers apart from Gemma. Nobody passes comment. The reflective circles of their lenses stare out from the sea wall. Unblinking eyes, endlessly watching.

The paramedics bag up the body and heave the stretcher up the beach, their feet slipping over the stones and driftwood that pockmark the sand. Gemma follows in their wake, leaving the two women and their children behind with a wave. The small boy waggles his spade back in response, sand flying in all directions. The two mothers nod their goodbye, faces ashen and blank. A noise flitters on the edge of her hearing. Carried and teased away by the wind. A tinny, empty clicking. Gemma looks up, sees the photographers training their lenses on the paramedics. Their fingers fluttering like a hummingbird's wings as they snap pictures over and over in synchronicity.

At the bottom of the steps, a female police officer stops Gemma. Tall and blonde, the woman's chin juts at a strange angle. "Thank you for your help today. It doesn't appear that the two women who found the body were in any fit state to call us. We offered them a ride home, but they seem content to pretend that nothing's happened."

"No problem. Happy to help. A terrible thing for children to see."

"In my experience, it's the children who heal quickest from these kinds of upsets. Anyway, we have your number and if we need anything else we'll be in touch."

The officer puts her hand across Gemma and guides her backwards so that her colleague can help the paramedics guide the stretcher up the steps. They struggle with the angle and with a few grunts, manage to swing the stretcher round and up to the ambulance. The female officer follows them up leaving Gemma alone on the sand. She looks up, trying to catch a glimpse of the photographers. She can't see them from this angle.

With a final glance back at the playing children, she bounds up the stairs to the top. A crowd stands in a half-moon around the ambulance and police car. Their blue lights circling but there are no sirens now there's no urgency to their journey. The damage is done. Their attendance purely administrative rather than life saving. People stand with their phones out, filming the scene or snapping pictures, calling friends to gossip.

The stone wall is deserted. The photographers are gone. Gemma pushes her way through the crowd, combing faces, trying to find the three men. She hurries, half jogging down the promenade. If they've broken from the crowd, they can't be far. She carries on her usual route, glancing into car windows as best she can without looking suspicious. At the end of the promenade, by the roundabout, she doubles back. Breaking into a full run, covering as much ground as she can, repeating the process of scanning cars, both parked and passing. Nothing. The three men have disappeared.

The ambulance and police car pull away somewhere behind her, starting their funereal march to the nearest morgue. The crowd disperses, people spilling back to their cars. Gemma stands and watches, daring the photographers to show themselves. She waits until her fingers go numb, and her nose begins to run. Then she turns and heads for home.

She breaks off from her online meeting, pushing her chair backwards from her desk. She stretches and stares out of the window at the drizzle splattering the window. Heavy enough to put most people off taking a walk but light enough to not stop her getting outside. After a morning of financial predictions and doom-mongering forecasts, the need for fresh air outweighs her need to stay dry. Slipping on her waterproof jacket, she locks the door and turns into the rain.

The chill of the day blasts through her sinuses. Thoughts of work freeze and shatter as she marches down sodden streets towards the seafront. Rivulets of rain pour across the pavements and into the gutter, threatening to numb her toes before she's even got started. Cars crackle past through the rain, brake lights reflecting in puddles. She puts her head down against the rain and strides towards the seafront.

It's busier than she'd like for a Wednesday lunchtime. Getting away from her screens and online meetings is only part of it. Not seeing people she knows or having to deal with any conversations for an hour is all she needs. Just the ability to keep to herself.

The supermarket car park is full. Builders in Hi-Viz vests barrelling in and out of the shops, grabbing lunch. A minibus unpacks its cache of elderly people, the driver helping them from the steps and carrying their wheeled, tartan shopping trollies. The town teems with life despite the weather's best attempts.

Gemma walks away from the shops, following her usual route out of town, down the promenade and back again. Murky brown sea steals her attention through the iron railings and over the top of the sea wall. She hops up, hands on the gravel concrete surface. The sea thrashes like a predator. Spray launches into the air further down the sea wall and she steps back, not wanting to get any wetter than she needs to. Head down against the onslaught of water. It's then she sees them.

The photographers stand on the sea wall, in their Sunday position. Three abreast. Wearing their same uniforms. The sight of them stops Gemma dead. Memories of the weekend were just that, something hideous that happened but required no further thought. No further emotional attachment or unpacking.

Their cameras are out and poised, pointing out to sea. Water surges against the sea wall sending an arc of spray over onto the promenade. The curve and power of it makes Gemma's breath catch in her throat but the photographers don't turn towards it. They make no effort to capture nature at its finest.

She bites the inside of her cheek. The intrusion into her day. The unwanted recollection of the weekend. How dare they? Their callousness in the face of a dead body and not only that, but to the trauma of the people involved. To stand and just take pictures, as children cried or as a corpse is bagged up and hauled away, there's something sick about that. Something inhuman. Barely one step up from those creeps outside nightclubs trying to take pictures up celebrities' skirts.

She stands behind them. Clears her throat. They don't turn round. She strains against the noise of the traffic but can't hear any clicks of photographs being taken. The photographers don't acknowledge her. They don't even acknowledge the weather, their hoods down, rain and seawater soaking into their hair and the exposed parts of their fleeces. Sodden patches bunch the knees of their slacks. But they don't move.

"Excuse me," she says. "Can I talk to you for a minute please?"

They don't move from their vigil on the seawall. Cold seeps up her back, spreading across her skin like water from a burst pipe. She doesn't have time for this. Doesn't need the aggravation or to waste part of her break bickering. But this isn't right. She reaches up, tugs at the jacket of the photographer in the middle.

At first, they don't move but then, as one, they swing round to face her. Their faces covered by their absurd, oversized lenses. She's unable to make out any features on their faces, just the edges. Retreating hairlines. Sagging loose skin on their necks. All of it window dressing for the vast glass circles prodding towards her face, reflecting her appearance back at her as she tries to find her voice.

"Can you move your cameras so I can talk to you properly please?" Her hands bunch in front of her, her legs half-turned in the direction of home.

They stand still. Mute. Cameras still in her face.

"Please?"

No response. Just three different angles of her own image in their lenses.

"Well," her hands find her hips. "What you did at the weekend, that wasn't right. Taking photos of a dead man like that. It's sick. I think you should delete them. You shouldn't be turning up at your little photography group or huddling over them in your dark rooms or whatever. It's not right."

Her voice trails off as the photographers stand still. Their lenses staring at her. No matter how she moves her head, she's unable to see their faces, unable to make eye contact. She takes a step back. Off to her left, there's a dinging sound. A bike bell. She turns to look at it. The same man as on Sunday. Luminous jacket. Black helmet. Water spraying from the wheels of his bike as he sluices down the pavement. He swerves round her, not looking at her or the photographers. She goes to call to him, to do what, to ask him for help? Unknown words freeze on her tongue.

The man rounds her, scoots past a man walking his dog and out onto the zebra crossing. Gemma reaches a hand out. She sees what he's missed. Too late. The builders' truck, unable to stop slams into the man. Skidding on the wet tarmac. His bike disappears under the wheels, causing the truck to wobble and skid. The man does the same, rolling into the black space beneath the grill. A gaping mouth beneath the windscreen. There's a thud and the scream of brakes.

Then a second of silence.

"Oh shit." She runs to the road, not even close to first on the scene. The dogwalker is on the phone, shouting for an ambulance. Shoppers are out of their cars, people lining the road, hands over mouths. One of the builders, the passenger, climbs down from the truck, looks beneath it and staggers away, hands behind his head. The driver remains in the cabin. His hands white on the steering wheel, his eyes searching the horizon for solace.

Gemma gets as close as she can, joining the group of people calling to the cyclist. They call to him, tell him it'll be okay, that help is coming. But as the group shifts and parts, Gemma catches a glimpse of him. He is nothing but meat.

She straightens up. Her vision wobbles and breaths don't come easily. She pulls out her inhaler and takes a long, cool puff on it. The medicine acts immediately and crisp air fills her lungs. She puts her hands on her knees, steadies herself. She can't be here. Can't do this again, not so soon after Sunday.

Straightening up, she steps backwards, out of the road, back onto the relative safety of the pavement. Mingling into the crowd, she backs away from the scene. Hand clutched to her chest as she hurries back towards her home. Her heart beats in her neck, thudding a tattoo beneath her eardrums.

She doesn't turn round when she hears it, but the sound makes her flinch, just as it did the weekend before. Her shoulders hunch, her arms tucked in. A defensive pose.

The vultures are out again.

Click, click, click, click, click.

She doesn't sleep that night. It takes days for the adrenaline to leave her system. The image of the cyclist's face, torn and crimson, appears behind her eyelids every time she blinks. She finds herself missing questions in meetings. Comments sailing over her head unnoticed as she sits and stares and loses herself in images she never wished to see.

She doesn't leave the house for a week. Not even at the weekend. She eats her lunch at her desk, skimming social media and twenty-four-hour news. She spends the weekend in a blur of old films and crappy American sitcoms that she knows off by heart. By the following Tuesday, she can't take anymore.

After her final morning meeting, she gets up, pushing her chair backwards across the wooden flooring where it spins away. Up the stairs, she throws on her gym kit and digs out her running trainers. It's been a while since she committed to a run, but she's built up so much energy being cooped up in the house that she can't think of a better outlet. It's either that or screaming her way through an afternoon meeting. She's got an hour. Time for a quick run, shower, and bite to eat. If she hurries. She slips her housekey off the bunch and lets herself out into the fresh air.

Running invigorates her, she completes a lap of her estate with ease. No burning calves or aching knees. Her afternoon meeting can stand to be a few minutes late. She steps out, upping the pace down the hill towards town. A cough lingers in her throat, but she shakes it off as she jogs past the high street and the supermarket. Not feeling self-conscious as she usually does. An old man sitting in his car in a disabled parking space watches her go over the top of his newspaper. Gemma smiles as his wife whacks him on the arm.

Down onto the promenade. That flat expanse of concrete. Beyond it, the sea toils away unseen. Its energy matching her own. Her breathing shortens, a tightness at the base of her ribs. She slows down and forces herself to speed up again, doing what she can to burn past the physical and mental barriers. Her shitty diet and even worse thoughts.

She makes it all the way to the end of the promenade for the first time in months. The seawall giving way to wrought iron railings. A strip of sand glows a dirty yellow in the meek sunlight. Brown water churns as the sea makes its way towards her again and again. She leans on the railing for a moment, trying to steady her breathing as it comes in thin, reedy bursts. Fatigue weighs heavy in her calves and she stretches them out, pushing the muscle to breaking point and letting go. It makes no difference as she starts the return trip.

She's almost at the photographers' usual spot when she notices they aren't there. She didn't even look on the way past. She doesn't slow, doesn't turn her head as she passes, just presses on for home. Her chest tightens further. The muscles between her ribs as hard as the bone they support. She pats her pockets as she runs. Her inhaler's sat on her desk with her phone. She'll be home soon. She can almost feel the cool hit of the medicine in her throat. Sweat sends a chill up her lower back.

Slowing down isn't an option, even as her breath rattles and wheezes through her chest. Cold air scalds the lining of her lungs. She presses on. Back past the supermarket and the shops. The incline digging its teeth into her leg muscles. A stitch jabs into her side. She slows. Her breathing more ragged now, a lack of rhythm. A lack of control.

She's in sight of her house now. Her vision closing in. Black lines frame everything she sees. Footsteps behind her. Scurrying over the concrete. She turns, bent double, and lets out a low moan.

They're here. The three of them. Lenses trained on her. Approaching from the other side of the road. They don't turn their lenses away from her as they step down from the kerb, scuttling across the street. Their sensible walking boots scrape the pavement as they close in.

She puts a hand up towards them, blocking her face from their view. They remain in her peripheral vision, hiding in the increasing black spots. Home is all that matters. The only thing she can see. She continues to run as best she can. Heading for the safety of the finish line.

Every breath a battle, her head swims as she enters her driveway. The scuffing of shoes behind her. So close she's sure she should be feeling their breath on her neck.

She takes another step and her leg trembles. Her hand plants against the car window but it offers no support. She's on her knees, slumped against the metal. Her ribs squeeze the air from her lungs and don't let anything back in.

The door is barely five yards away, but the detail is draining from her vision. The number blurred against the red paint. A photograph losing contrast and focus. The aperture closing, blackness taking up so much of her vision.

Those familiar scurrying footsteps. A lens in her face. Her vision closes to a pin prick, the aperture shutting out light for good. One final sound as her attempt at a breath gains no purchase.

Click.

THE RIDER

BRIAN EVENSON

I.

WHEN HIS CAR began to rattle and smoke, Reiter managed to force his way across the lanes of traffic to pull up against the concrete wall. He waited there for someone to stop and help him, but no one did. Then he waited for a break in traffic so as to safely climb out. He almost had his door taken off when he finally did open it, and then there he was, standing with his back pressed to his car, as, horns blaring, cars roared past a mere handsbreadth away.

Holding his breath, he sidled down the body of the car until he finally made it around to the front, where it was safe. He opened the hood and stared at the ticking machinery inside, but nothing seemed obviously wrong.

He waited for the police or a tow truck to arrive, but neither did. As the sun started to set, he began walking down the side of the freeway. Cars flew past in a regular swishing motion, the sound almost hypnotic, sometimes coming near enough to make him afraid. For a dozen minutes or so he kept walking along the concrete wall, but eventually the wall became a chain link fence. The fence was too high to climb: he had to keep walking until, finally, he came to a section where the mesh had come loose near the bottom, leaving a ragged gap.

On the other side lay an expanse of barren land, barely visible in the growing dark. A little way beyond that, he saw a dim scattering of houses, a town of some sort. It would be an easy matter, he told himself, to make his way down there, find someone who could direct him to a phone, and call a tow truck. And so, he forced the wire mesh up as best he could and squirmed his way through.

And now, here he was. He made his stumbling way down the slope, which was steeper than it had initially looked and difficult to navigate in the gathering dark. He ended up wading into a stretch of prickly scrub, had to turn and try to stumble his way around it. But at last he had reached the bottom, his shoes half-full of powdery dirt, and could step over a low stone wall onto a cobbled street.

He straightened his jacket, dusted off his trousers. Sitting on the stone wall he removed a shoe, shook the dirt out of it, put it back on. Then he did the same with the other shoe.

Only then did he look around. He was apparently in a residential district, no signs for businesses—none that were illuminated anyway. There were streetlights, feeble and yellow, and somehow suspended so far up in the air as to illuminate little at ground level. What town was this? Hapsworth? Chatsmith? He didn't remember there being a historic town along the route—all the towns found out this way were newer, sprung up weedlike in the last decade or two. But clearly there must have been one he'd missed. He had left his map in the car so couldn't check.

With a sigh he rose and started walking.

He walked down a cobbled street, planning to knock at the first house with lights on inside of it, wanting to find someone that he wouldn't bother too much if he knocked on their door. But there were no lit windows, everything was dark. The street too was deserted: there was not a single person or animal in sight. He reached the end of the cobbled street and turned on to another street, also cobbled, and found that to be deserted as well: nobody afoot, no moving or parked cars, no pets, no crows, nothing but dark, seemingly deserted houses. It felt to him almost like a film set, as if these houses had never been meant to be occupied. Even the trash on the street seemed carefully crumpled and deposited, as if actual humans had had no part in leaving it there. And the smell was wrong too. Or rather there *was* no smell—that was what was wrong.

He chose a door at random and knocked on it, then waited. There was a moment where he thought he might have heard a rustling coming from deep within, but perhaps he merely imagined this. In any case, even though he waited and knocked again, then knocked a third time, the house remained dark and the door did not open.

He tried the next door, and the next. Same result. *Do I just keep trying doors?* he wondered. *When do I admit to myself that something is wrong?*

He pushed such thoughts down. What good did it do him to think them? Hardmill? Jettlesford? Maybe a name a little like that, like one of those. Or maybe a combination of the two. If he squinted his mind hard enough, he could almost imagine seeing a little dot labelled *Hardford* on his missing map.

He knocked on the next door, then saw that there was a bell. That was different. He felt vaguely cheered by this, and rang it.

Was it overkill to ring it even though he'd just knocked? Apparently not, since nobody answered.

He tried a dozen more doors, following no particular logic, no particular pattern. He would try two or three in a row, then walk a half block, then try another. No lights were ever on, none came on when he knocked or rang, nobody ever answered. His feet were beginning to ache now. He was hearing a faint, low humming, a buzzing almost, that might be coming from the street lights, though he couldn't be sure. *Beetlesbury?* he wondered. *Carcosalia?* Each street seemed nearly identical to the last, same row of semi-detached houses, doors all the same mustard yellow, same trash even—so at least it began to seem to him: a crumpled, sodden page of a newspaper swirling in the filthy water of a backed-up gutter, a scattering of old grimy confetti from some long-dead holiday, a banana's blackened half-peel. Could he trace his way back the way he had come, climb the hill, squeeze through the fence, and get back to his car? He wasn't sure. He had become, perhaps, more confused than he had realized. Not planning to go back, he hadn't marked his route. Besides, would his car even be there when he got back? Wasn't it likely it had been towed away by now? And then there he would be: stuck on the freeway with cars roaring past.

Spatchcocklesford? Flaysville? Ridiculous! No, it couldn't be something like that. Who would name a town that! And yet he couldn't escape the impression that the name was just there, on the tip of his tongue, that the blank spot on the map in his mind's eye was just on the verge of beginning to fill.

He reached the end of another cobbled street and turned onto the next cobbled street, then stopped dead. There, midway down the block, at last, was a house with its windows lit.

II.

The house had a bell as well as a knocker. He hesitated over which he should use. Did it matter? Probably not, but it felt to him like it should, like it was a test of some kind, and that if he chose wrong the door wouldn't open. After all, no doors had opened for him yet.

In the end, he rang with his right hand and knocked with his left, as if there were more than one person at the door. Then he waited.

For a long moment, nothing happened. Should he have rung with his left and knocked with his right? He pressed his ear against the door and listened, but heard nothing.

And then, suddenly, the door swung open. He jerked back. There, standing in the crack, was a somewhat dazed-looking man. Sitting on his shoulders, the top of his head cut off by the top of the door frame, was a small boy, maybe five or six years old. He had one hand pressed to the side of the man's face. The other was anchored in the hair on the top of the man's head.

Father and son, he thought. *Playing together. How sweet.*

"I'm sorry," Reiter said. "I can see I'm interrupting a game."

"Game?" said the man. His voice was thick, slow. His eyes droopy.

"You're not interrupting," said the young boy. His voice on the other hand was almost preternaturally high. *Perhaps it has just been too long since I have been around a child,* thought Reiter.

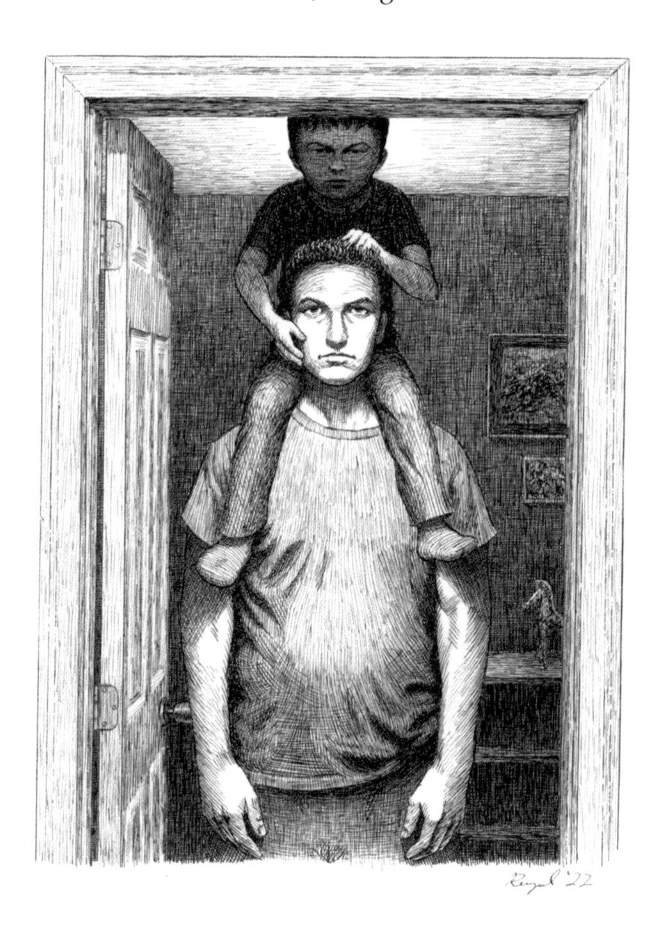

"I'm sorry to bother you," he said again. "If I could just use your phone," he said. "My car, you see."

"Your car?" said the man.

"A breakdown. I'll call the tow truck, be out of your hair."

"Hair?"

"Please," said the young boy. Apart from the pitch of his voice, he sounded older than he was. "Do come in."

The man lurched back to make space for him. The boy must have gripped his hair more firmly to keep from falling off, because the man's chin shot up so that it looked like he was staring at the ceiling. He shuffled awkwardly back, all the time the boy's other hand pressed to the side of his head.

"Is your father all right?" he asked the boy.

The boy laughed. "He's not my father," he said.

"No?" If not his father, what, then, had he interrupted?

"Does he not seem all right?"

"Frankly, no," Reiter said. And then added, "No offense."

The boy shrugged. "It's just ... what did you call it?"

"Excuse me?"

"When you first came in? The thing you worried you were interrupting."

He stared at the boy. "A ... game?" he finally said.

"Game," said the man.

"Yes," the boy said. "That. I'll remember it now. But you're not interrupting. You can be part of it too."

Part of what? Reiter wondered. He opened his mouth to speak, but before he could the man lumbered toward him. He flinched away and to the side, only to see that the man was not coming toward him after all, but just shutting the door.

"Don't want to let the cold seep in," said the boy.

"Seep in," echoed the man.

"Right," Reiter said. "Don't want to waste gas."

"Gas ," said the man, the boy's hand still pressed firmly to his cheek.

And then the boy lifted his hand away and scratched his own neck. The man below him fell stock still and then he began to shiver all over, and then he uttered a hoarse scream.

Quickly the boy's hand slapped itself against the side of the man's face again. Immediately he fell silent. A moment later, his shaking stopped.

"What's wrong with him?" asked Reiter.

"He just likes me to touch him," said the boy. "It's nothing to be concerned about."

"But you already had your hand knotted in his hair."

"Hair doesn't count," explained the boy. "It's dead."

Reiter was not sure what to say to that. He cleared his throat. "If I could just use the phone," he said, "I'll get out of your..."

"Hair," said the man.

Reiter swallowed, nodded.

"I should have been clear," said the boy. "We don't have a ... phone." He said *phone* as if it were a foreign word, a kind of wind.

"Hair!" said the man again proudly.

"Yes," said the boy, smiling. "Hair. Clever fellow!" He turned to Reiter. "I'm still not being clear," said the boy. "We can take you to a *phone*, but we were just sitting down for dinner. We'll take you right after we're done."

Reiter hesitated, nodded.

"But of course you'll eat with us," said the boy. "There's plenty."

Once again Reiter hesitated, and then once again he nodded. What alternative was there?

The table was already set, but just for two, the two places right beside one another. A tureen of what looked like some sort of goulash steamed in the rectangular table's center. Slowly the boy and the man he was riding left the room and then returned with another plate and a setting. They placed them on the opposite side of the table.

"Please," said the boy, "sit."

Reiter, reluctantly, did. He watched the man pull out the chair and settle into it, the boy still perched on his shoulders. Only once he was fully settled did the boy clamber down. When he did, Reiter now noticed, he never let go of the man, was always touching his exposed skin. When the boy finally took his seat next to the man, he was holding the man's hand.

The boy looked at Reiter. "Please," he said. "Help yourself."

Reiter reached out, took the ladle, dipped it, poured it into his bowl.

"Don't be modest," said the boy. And so Reiter, though he wasn't sure what the goulash was, or even if it was goulash, poured another ladlesworth into his bowl.

Ladlesworth, thought Reiter. *Bowlford?* He shook his head to clear it. Across from him the man had filled his bowl and had already begun to eat, spoon held awkwardly in the hand the boy wasn't holding, his mouth slurping the goulash, if it was goulash, off his spoon. The boy's bowl, on the other hand, remained empty.

"You're not going to eat?" asked Reiter.

"Don't you worry about me," said the boy. "I'll be fine."

And indeed the body did look fine. His color was good even though the man beside him seemed to grow more and more pale despite all the food he shoveled in. Reiter lifted his spoon, stared at the soup in it, and then placed the spoon back in the bowl. There were, he saw now, strange marks on the side of the man's head where the boy had pressed his hand, and when the man turned a little and the light caught them he saw they were little stipplings of blood.

"Good soup," the man said, to nobody in particular.

"Yes," said the boy. "Very good."

"I should leave," said Reiter.

"But you just got here!" said the boy. "Please, eat."

"Got here," said the man. His voice was weaker now, and he seemed very pale. The boy, by contrast, had grown positively florid. His hand remained closed very tightly over the man's hand.

Reiter stood.

"If you just point me in the direction I need to walk to find a phone, that will be enough for me," he said.

"Too much," said the man. Slowly, lazily, he let the spoon slip from his fingers. It clattered against the table's edge and down onto the floor. And then the man fainted.

"Help me," said the boy.

"Is he all right?" asked Reiter.

The boy shrugged. "If you help me, we can carry him into the bedroom."

But Reiter hesitated, didn't come around to the other side of the table.

"Is he still breathing?" asked Reiter finally. "Shouldn't we call an ambulance?"

"No telephone," said the boy. "Remember?"

"We can lay him flat on the floor and go out to call them."

"He'll be fine," said the boy. "Probably." And then he let go of the man's hand and stretched his hand across the table toward Reiter. Where he had been touching the man's hand, Reiter saw, it was smeared with blood.

"What's going on here?" asked Reiter. "What's really going on?"

The boy shrugged. "It's just ... a game," he said, turning the word around on his tongue, tasting it. "It just went a little too far."

"A game?" said Reiter, his voice rising. "I don't want to play." And then he turned and strode toward the door.

Or started to anyway. The boy was quick, and by the time he was nearly to the end of his side of the table, the boy was to the end of his own side. Reiter stopped and reversed course and then, seeing the boy nearly upon him, began to run. The boy turned and ran the other way and so Reiter reversed course as well, keeping the table between them. Soon he was out of breath.

They stood glaring at one another across the table, the mans' body still slouched in its chair.

"I thought you didn't want to play," said the boy. He didn't seem at all short of breath. "And yet we're having such fun!"

"Let me go," said Reiter. "Please."

The boy gestured behind him. "There's the door," he said. "What's keeping you?"

It was silly, he tried to tell himself. He shouldn't be afraid of a little boy. The bloody stippling on the man's neck was dried blood, probably, and he'd wanted the boy to put his hand on it to comfort him, to protect a wound, that was all. And the blood on the man's hand had come from that as well, from him pressing his own hand to his abraded neck. That was all. There was nothing to worry about, he told himself, nothing at all.

But he couldn't quite believe it.

The man groaned, began to stir.

"You see?" said the boy, "no ambulance needed. "He'll be fine. I take care of my chattel."

"Your what?"

"Is that the wrong word?" he shrugged. "My friend, I meant to say." He turned to Reiter. "We're all friends here aren't we?"

The boy waited for an answer, but Reiter said nothing.

"Have it your way," the boy said. The man groaned again, moving his head a little, and the boy, making little calming noises, the kinds of noises you might use to settle a household pet you had accidentally stepped on, took a few steps toward him.

Immediately Reiter rushed toward the door, but he'd estimated wrong. The boy was even quicker than he'd been led to believe, particularly now, since he had fallen onto all fours and was galloping forward. Suddenly Reiter wasn't sure it was even a boy at all. He almost opened the door, even firmly grasped the knob, but before he could turn it, he felt the boy's hand, if hand was really the right word for it, close around his other wrist.

He felt a brief, very sharp pain, and then a numbness began to spread up his arm. When, a moment later, his other hand tried to turn the knob, he found it wouldn't move at all. His whole body wouldn't move, he realized, none of it.

The numbness in his arm spread everywhere, bringing along with it a pleasant, peaceful feeling. Even the room felt brighter. He felt the boy clambering up his body like a monkey, one appendage always kept pressed to his bare flesh. He felt as well, as if from a great distance, the boy reach his hand and take hold of his hair. Then he could see the boy's knees on either side of his head. The boy was riding him.

And then suddenly Reiter was moving, though not of his own volition. The boy was doing it. He felt at a great distance his hand release the knob of the door. He felt his body turn and plod back into the room. He saw his arms reach out and grab hold of the other man, and then they dragged him out of the chair and toward a door in the far wall.

The door did not lead, as Reiter had been led to expect, to a bedroom. It was more like a closet, except for the fact that each wall except for the wall with the door had a set of iron chains and cuffs.

He watched from within himself as the boy directed his body with care, as it caused him to lean the semiconscious and groaning body of the man against one wall, then held him there as it attended to affixing the cuffs and clicking them shut.

"Very good," said the boy. "You're a natural."

"Natural," he heard his voice slur out.

He tried to run, but his body wouldn't move at all. Or, rather, would only move when the boy told it to.

"We'll save him," said the boy as he forced Reiter's body to shut the door. "We'll keep him for when you need a break from the *game*. You can take turns."

"Turns," said Reiter.

And then, with a slight flexion of his palm, the boy led him out of the closet that was not a closet and out into the rest of his admittedly short life.

THE SHADOW OF HIS BONES

J.T. BUNDY

ENGLAND WAS COLD AND WET, glimmers of night traffic visible from above. Ben had caught the last plane before the travel corridors closed and spent the flight in a narcotic stupor: part dream, part hallucination. He retained snatches of the journey—seat buckle, headrest, the altitude sound in his ears—with only a dim sense of the disaster unfolding in the skies outside. As they taxied to land, the white noise of the cabin had almost lulled him to sleep. But then he was at the chaos of border control with no memory of leaving the aircraft.

"You're one of the lucky ones," said the young staffer at the desk. She stared through him, as if visualising the cloud of volcanic ash as it spread towards the continent. "This whole thing has been a nightmare."

"Yes."

Now she was flicking through his passport. "That'll be the last route for, like, *a while*."

For a moment he was incandescent with rage, like he might scream in her face. Instead, he thrust out his hand. "Are we done?"

"Of course." She laid the passport in his palm.

Then he felt guilty. "My father died."

"Oh. I'm sorry to hear that."

"Don't be. It wasn't much of a surprise."

His name was Ray, he wanted to tell her, but he was already being waved along.

Everything was woozy and unreal. The airline had lost his bags, so he went empty-handed to the train station. He wasted several minutes squinting at the departures board with black light in his periphery. Nearby, a group had formed around a plasma screen. Above the headline *NO FLY ZONE* was live feed of the eruption, a stygian column of smoke streaked with great arcs of lightning. "They're turning people away at Schiphol, Charles de Gaulle," someone commented. "The steam from the glacier made it so much worse," said another. Further along, a rail worker was directing the flow of people in tones approaching serenity. Ben saw she'd left her body a while ago. He sympathised.

He queued for about an hour, then boarded the train. The carriage was chaotic, stacked luggage and passengers in the aisles. He was shame incarnate as he clambered through; his rumpled suit, his journey-smell. Somehow, he found a spot in the vestibule, but the feelings of wrongness wouldn't leave him. He fingered his armpit, rubbed his bloodshot eyes, tugged a roll of stomach flab until it hurt. *Grotesque,* he thought, *you're so fucking grotesque . . .*

He closed his eyes.

Deep breath.

The vestibule.

The rock of the carriage.

When he opened them again, he saw a passenger stood opposite him, a prim woman boxed in by suitcases. She had a gentle hand on his shoulder. "Are you unwell?"

"My father died," he explained, believing it more the second time.

"Heavens," she replied. "My condolences."

"Noted."

Yes, Ray had been sick for a very long time. Among other things, there were problems with his lungs. Pleural effusion, it was called, fluid retention in the tissue. At first, Ben had been the dutiful son, accompanying his father to his appointments without complaint. All until the chest drain. Scalpel incision. Needle between the ribs. Bloodied runoff spattering into the collection bottle. Ray hadn't seemed bothered, or to even feel it at all—only relief when he could breathe again. But Ben had been terrified. And it wasn't only the disease. Incessant injury. Cognitive decline. Nose-blind to the stench of your own urine. If these were the consequences of age, you could count him out.

Livia's martyr complex had taken on the rest. Ben was happy for his sister to shoulder the burden—he'd rather crawl into a hole and die than set foot in a hospital again. And from then on, it was easy to find reasons not to visit Ray. Because that was just as *Gorno* had taken off.

The film had been in gestation for over a decade, shot in fits and starts between a string of dead-end jobs. But by late 2009, Ben was finally touting his baby on the horror festival circuit: Glasgow, Manchester, Brussels. The feature received moderate buzz, some minor prizes; the judges praised a "lurid little shocker in the Cronenberg mould." But no distribution deal. He cloistered himself in rented apartments as he contemplated a life without meaning—almost 40 years old with no career and no prospects. Then, around springtime, the call finally came. Clémence Sangier, a prominent figure in the New French Extremity, was in America workshopping her Hollywood debut. She'd been impressed with the micro-budget ingenuity of *Gorno* and was interested in meeting its director. Could Ben fly to LA to discuss his future? Of course—he'd jumped on the first plane. But then he'd languished by the motel pool for what felt like eternity. "Naturally, we're *very* curious to meet you," said Sangier's producer with customary Gallic indifference, "but sadly we must delay." A couple of days, max. Then one week became two . . .

And now Ray was gone.

Of course, Livia had been there when it happened: *Dad went in the night. I wish I could say it was peaceful. He was trying to tell me something, but I've no idea what.* The messages had been typical of her—predisposed to enigma. But maybe the old man did have secrets after all.

Ben was dreaming on his feet when his BlackBerry rang.

"Speak of the devil."

"When do you arrive? I thought you'd be here by now."

"Jesus, Livia, do you even watch the news?"

"Sure I do. The volcano. What's it called? Eyja . . . Eyjafja . . ."

"It's not worth the attempt. Believe me."

Then she got flustered. "It's just that I've got so much to sort out—the funeral, the flowers, the probate, his accounts—and the hospital's saying he needs an autopsy, because of his time in the Navy. That means there's the coroner to deal with as well, the paperwork, the inquest in the courts." She was always like this over the phone—

mildly hysterical, information delivered at speed. "What I'm saying is I might not be able to collect you when you get into town."

"I'll make my own way."

"And the house is a state, you should find a hotel."

"It's fine. How bad can it be?"

"I'd really rather you found a room."

"Don't be ridiculous. I'm happy anywhere. I'll sleep on the fucking floor if I have to." He cleared some congestion in his nose. "I really don't care either way."

There was a moment's silence on the line.

"Ben, have you taken something?"

"What's that got to do with anything?"

"So, you admit it."

"I needed some benzos for the flight. So what?" He played with the pills in his pocket. "They don't even work. I feel like if I don't sleep soon, I'm going to hurt somebody."

Now she was getting upset. "Don't you even care he's dead?"

"Come on, Liv."

"That's not an answer."

"Look, he was my dad too."

"Believe me, I know. The prodigal son returns. Only a little too late."

His heart started to race, but he let it go. Their relationship couldn't handle an argument right now. They'd fought over the film since the premiere. He supposed the autobiographical parts were too blatant to ignore.

"Listen, Ben—"

"We're going into a tunnel," he said quickly. "Speak tomorrow."

"No, wait—"

He hung up.

The woman across from him avoided his gaze. "I haven't cried for a decade," he told her. "And I'm not about to start now."

She said something in reply as they entered the tunnel, but Ben couldn't hear her over the roar of the train. Instead, he turned towards the window and watched the darkness rushing past. He put his hand on the glass. He closed his eyes.

From the street, the house had an evacuated look: open curtains and darkness within. As he went around the back, where the door was unlocked, a text from Livia pinged through. *Hope you got there safe. Sorry for what I said before. And about the house. Like I said, it's a mess. Oh, and one thing—*

He took off his shoes and went inside.

After Mum died, Ray had let the place fall into disorder. Ben took in the used mugs and bowls, the piled junk mail and magazine subscriptions, the sixpacks of cider that marked the journey between rooms (the old man drank to vent—the whole family did). He even found cigarettes inside the bread bin, a discovery that enraged him until he took one from the box and it crumbled to flakes in his palm. In that regard, the house was much the same as his last visit. But something had changed in the intervening months. Now Ray's illnesses had taken over everything.

Dosing cassettes: lozenges, capsules, and tablets. Medical consumables: bandages and adult diapers. And equipment everywhere—a heart monitor, a blood pressure cuff, devices for palliative care. But most prominent was the oxygenator. The instrument had pride of place on the living room rug. Ben jiggled the cable until the flow *whooshed* online. He inserted the nostril tubing and snorted—the enriched air made him giddy. Then, as he found his balance, he stepped into wet carpet. "Fuck me," he said as the liquid soaked into his socks. Only then did the rest of Livia's message arrive. *One thing. For the love of God, don't take off your shoes.*

He went upstairs.

Ray had slept in his recliner towards the end, so the main bedroom hadn't been used for some time. There was a mirror propped against the bed, and a brighter oval of paintwork where it had been removed from the wall. Within it was a stain in the plaster, irregular in shape and variously discoloured. *Like a bruise,* Ben thought.

He re-hung the mirror to cover the mark. Then he looked himself over. Everything was wrong: rank asymmetry, deviated septum, the stippled remainder of teenage acne. And now something new, a skin tag in the crease of his eyelid. There would be nail scissors in the bathroom—sharp, precise, useful for minor surgeries. But you had to be careful. You could get carried away. One time, slicing off a mole had led to several stitches in the hospital. Because once you started, you had to keep digging to get it all . . .

He rode the stairlift down, just for the hell of it.

There was a strange, quiet atmosphere as the night wore on. Eventually, he found himself in the dining room. To his right was the screen door into the conservatory. You couldn't see into the garden beyond, only the mirroring of the room behind him in the interior light. He appraised his shape one more time. Then, for a second, he swore the old man's reflection appeared beside his own. Ray was just as he saw him last: wattles at his neck and a pendulous sag in the groin. Only this time his eyes were shut, his face was pale as a death mask, and his hands were raised in fright like he was trapped in the glass.

He scrambled for his phone, but by the time he looked up, Ray was gone.

"Jet-lag," he said to nobody. "Mental exhaustion. Or the pills."

But it had seemed so real.

He turned on the TV. A backwater channel was showing re-runs of *Extreme Surgeries*. The main event was a filmed breast reconstruction. Next up was a regulation rhinoplasty, but he was asleep by the time the procedure commenced.

He woke up, clicked off the set, and trudged upstairs.

The bedroom was in darkness. Reaching across the wall, he found something malleable where the light switch should be. He left it alone and risked the void with shivers running down his spine.

Safe in bed, the frame shrieked under his weight, so he laid still and stared at the walls. After a while, the eerie quiet had returned. As consciousness faded, he braced himself to hear Ray's voice, or to see his hunched silhouette at the door. But nothing happened.

Soon he fell asleep with the scissors in his hand.

The next morning, Ben was in the bathroom when Livia arrived. There was glass everywhere, piled on the shower seat like turquoise snow. He brushed some of the shards into a dustpan and stood up.

"What the hell happened here?" she asked him. "Take a sledgehammer to the place?"

"The door blew up in the middle of the night. You should've heard it. I came running out onto the landing before I was even awake." His lip quivered. "I'm a little freaked out."

"Yeah, they do that. It's the tempered glass. Microscopic defects, or something. It just goes."

Ben mulled that over. Then he looked at his sister, who he hadn't seen for a long time. There was an aura of tired acceptance about her, of ageing enforced by circumstance.

She voiced it for the both of them. "He'd been sick forever."

"Longer than he'd been healthy."

"Yeah."

They hugged.

"We're orphans," she said into his chest.

"Pretty sure there's an age limit on that."

"Probably."

They separated.

"You know, I think I saw him," he said.

"What?"

"Dad. Last night, in the screen door."

"Don't bring your weird energy in here, please. The situation's bad enough."

"Sorry."

She was absent for a moment, staring at the moisture on the bathroom tiles, the laughter-line cracks in the ceiling. Then she clapped her hands on his shoulders. "OK, time to get to work. First things first, let's open a window. I can't breathe in here." She looked him up and down. "And you need a change of clothes. I brought Mark's for you to wear."

Her husband. "He doesn't mind?"

"He doesn't need them anymore," she said obliquely. "Unless you prefer Dad's wardrobe?"

"Are you kidding? I wouldn't be seen dead— Ouch!"

He'd cut his finger on the glass. It had already started to bleed.

"Here," Livia said. "Let me."

She took his hand and nursed the wound in her mouth. Just like when they were kids.

They cleaned out the house over the next few days. First, they sorted through all the shopping-channel gadgets—the steam cleaners, foot massagers, and meat-roasting thermometers—that Ray had hoarded over the years. Next, the impromptu repairs that had occupied the rest of his time: stripped electronics and abandoned refurbishments. At one point, they found an older model of the oxygenator, its nitrogen scrubber removed and dismantled. Then, atop some withered napery on the dining room table, the exploded-view components of a microwave. Ben looked at the metal casings, the magnetron as centrepiece. "This doesn't seem very safe," he called over his shoulder.

Livia shrugged. "He liked to know how things worked."

Underneath were correspondence related to the exposure claim. As a veteran of nuclear testing, tinkering with a source of electromagnetic radiation was the last thing their father should've been doing; there was a reason the kids at school called him "Gamma Ray." But the doctors took a more relaxed view. They gave the same answer as when he was found supplementing his daily morphine with rum—a man in his condition could do entirely as he pleased.

Livia saw him with the letters.

"The campaign's going nowhere," she said.

"For the medal? Fat lot of good that's going to do him now. What about the class action?"

Because it wasn't only the bomb. Back then, Naval ships used asbestos for everything: fireproofing, water resistance, corrosive protection. "The fibres were everywhere," she said. "In the paint, the flooring, the insulation. They wore anti-flash hoods during artillery drills—full of the stuff. It was even in their bedding."

"I suppose they didn't know," said Ben. But he didn't believe it. Asbestos in the air, asbestos in their lungs. *They knew.*

Livia went home in the evening, but there were still Ray's medical records to organise. Ben took a pill, slumped on the sofa, and picked at the leftovers of their takeaway. The TV was all talent shows and stuff about the general election. Otherwise, the news was still dominated by the ash cloud, depicted as a black smudge covering much of the Northern Hemisphere. An aviation specialist was prophesying doom: melted glass in the engines, abrasion to the fuselage. Next up was an item about the volcano itself, located at the bottom tip of the Icelandic *Suðurland*. "With only twenty thousand inhabitants, this remote area straddles a plate boundary of intense geothermal activity . . ."

Ben went through the boxes—mostly doctor's notes and physiotherapy logs. But one was full of radiology reports. He looked through all the ghost images that had been taken of Ray over the years. Bone scintigraphs with radionuclide tracers (Ben remembered his lost luggage, his clothes in spectral view inside the baggage scanner). Chest exams showing the shadow on the lungs (the ash cloud, the plume of black smoke). On screen, the experts spoke of volcanic quiescence, the hibernation between eruptions. But all Ben could think of was the plane leaving the runway, the lurch in his stomach as it banked in the air . . .

He opened his eyes and saw the oxygenator humming at his feet. He drew air from the high flow mask and thought some more about his father. Then he fell asleep that way, his breath fogging the plastic.

The funeral was a neutral affair, neither sombre nor joyful. The celebrant—an odd, unshaven man whose eccentricities could not be blamed on religion—had kept it brief and secular. Nevertheless, Ben had a deep distrust of ceremony, so had borne the whole thing with his nails dug into his arm. In fact, he'd been like this since leaving the house, muscles tensed and easily startled. But Ray was finally gone, cremated and conveyed into the air. So why did he still feel this way? All this adrenaline coursing through him—in readiness for what?

After the wake, Livia needed some time to herself, and Ben supposed he did too. He tried to keep busy.

Home was a satellite town without much going for it, a suburban sprawl built over landfill and an airfield used during the war. The next morning, Ben woke before dawn, left the house, and started walking with no destination in mind. He toured the shopping precinct, the library, the leisure centre that had seen better days. Then the estates themselves, the modest streets and identikit developments, the indistinguishable lives. No change was permitted here. Only homogenous growth, expansion of the same. *And there's a word for that,* he thought. *Cancer.*

Yes, the old resentments were surfacing again. And the siblings had always clashed about the divide. "Cities are broken places for people trying to disappear," Livia liked to say. "But out here you can't hide from yourself." It was hard to argue with that.

He reached the rec ground and sat for a while under the ageing pavilion. When he was a child, the carnival had passed through here—the Wurlitzer, the carousel, the haunted train. Even at that age, he'd been disturbed by crowds, so Ray had sheltered him inside the funhouse. But the mirrors—the ballooning distortions in the coloured lights—had sent him into a panic. Confronted by disturbing, homuncular reflections at every turn, he'd started to cry. Then Ray's patience had worn thin. "Get a hold of yourself," he'd said with his hand against the glass. "It's nothing—just a trick of the light."

Once around the town was enough. Then Ben decided to get drunk.

He spent a couple of hours in one of the local pubs until his position became untenable. Then the bouncer, stone-faced and unreceptive, escorted him onto the pavement. There was golden light behind the houses and a wake of red kites in orbit above. But no planes, he noticed, no contrails in the sky.

Staggering on, he collided with a pregnant woman taking the air. "Oh my gosh, are you *alright?*" she said like he was some kind of imbecile.

"I'm fine."

"No seriously,"—she ducked to find his eyes—"did I *hurt* you?"

"What the hell are you talking about?"

She chuckled at that, then started unwrapping some gum. "Nicotine. Want some?" She popped it into her mouth.

"You'll poison your baby," he said, not caring how she took it.

She gave him a dead-eyed look. "It's better than the alternative." Then she got playful all of a sudden, smoothing her belly. "Want to feel?"

"Really?"

"Everybody does."

She took his hand and placed it on the bump. He could sense it immediately—the total bliss of the womb.

"How long?" he asked.

"Not long," she replied. "And it's a pair."

"My sister was a twin. She absorbed our brother in the first trimester. Poor guy never had a chance."

"Gnarly."

Ben spread his fingers. Press a little harder and her belly would dimple. *But imagine squeezing. Imagine pushing your fingers right through the skin.*

They locked eyes.

"Do we know each other?" she asked.

"No."

"Didn't we go to school together?"

"Maybe. But I look different now."

"No, no . . . I remember you." She grinned. "Really, you haven't changed a— Holy shit!"

Something was sidewinding across the road.

"It's a fucking snake!" said Ben, backing against the pub exterior.

"It's not a snake. It's a slow worm. A legless lizard."

She said it like he understood the distinction. Then the creature was in the gutter, tracking through the leaves and heading for the drain.

Ben was shaken up now. "How could something so disgusting be allowed to live?"

As the worm made its way into the sewer system, the woman stared into the middle distance and laughed again. "The Lord works in mysterious ways. Man, I need a cigarette."

Ben spent the next morning decontaminating the bedrooms. The rest of the day he stood looking mournfully at the sky. The travel ban was still in effect as, almost a week since the eruption, the volcano continued to pump mineral ash into the European weather system. He checked his phone again. There'd been a couple of emails from the producer's office overnight. When could he get back stateside? Soon, right? Because it was not wise to keep Mme. Sangier waiting . . .

He loped downstairs. Livia was sat on the rug with photographs spread before her. She passed one to him. "Their wedding day."

He held the photo of his parents in the light. They were smiling in a way that seemed totally alien to him.

"A couple of days before he died," Livia said, "he told me he thought Mum was still in the house."

"What do you mean?"

"I think it must've been dementia finally getting to him, because he'd talked about it before, people moving around at night. I told him he was probably dreaming."

"Or strung out on all the meds." Ben was sifting through patient leaflets, a litany of side effects and interactions. "Look at what they were giving him. Vasodilators, blood thinners, mood stabilisers, diuretics. And I haven't even got to the stronger stuff. I can hardly pronounce the names of some of these. No wonder he was seeing things."

"Maybe."

"Maybe?"

She went back to the photos. "Mum always said you were the spit of each other." There was one of Ray in his navy whites. "See? The resemblance is uncanny."

Ben snorted. "We look nothing alike." And his father was a preening man delighted by his own company. No, there was no comparison.

"For sure. It's in the cranium. And the morose expression in the eyes." She inclined her head to consider the photo some more. "Handsome, of course . . . in the right lighting. Are you seeing anybody right now?"

"Women aren't exactly beating down my door."

"Why not? You're a fine specimen."

"Specimens belong in formaldehyde."

"I can't talk to you when you're like this."

He knelt down next to her. There was a stack of other files from Ray's Naval career. He'd enlisted as a teenager in the summer of 1950. Seven years later he was out in the Pacific. Livia was looking at an aerial photo of the island where he'd been stationed, a wishbone of white sand around an azure lagoon. But the bomb test had been out in open water. "They weren't given protective equipment to watch it go off," she said. "They just lined them up on the boat and told them to cover their eyes. No wonder they all . . ." She froze with suppressed frustration.

"They got sick, Liv. You can say it."

She swerved the thought and carried on. "Even with their backs turned, the explosion was so bright he could see right through his hands. He saw—what did he call it?"

Ben knew. "The shadow of his bones."

He'd tried to imagine what it was like. The phosphorescent brilliance of the detonation. A thunder-crack like the sky tearing open. The rose glow of the light through his skin. Then, after a delay of distance, the heatwave—sunburn warmth and his hair blown back in the gale. And it was true: by now, all of Ray's peers were in the ground. Patrick Binding. Harry Case. Arthur "Sweat" Lodge. Many had succumbed quickly to the effects of the radiation, the shadow cast by the mushroom cloud. Others had met more violent ends, beset by crippling headaches and personality changes. Yes, the testing had laid a curse on all of their families. Rare malignancies in the men. Miscarriages in their wives. And congenital deformity in the children that made it to term—twisted spines, cleft palates, missing limbs (or only the bones). What else? Duplex kidneys. Crystals in the urine. Two sets of teeth fighting for space in the jaw. All of it visited upon the innocent. And all of it ignored—the calls for compensation refused, the link between illness and exposure denied.

"He suffered so much," she said. "Why do people carry on?"

"There's a drive, I guess."

Still the question went unsaid. Ray had married late in life and had children even later. To him, the siblings had been no more than an afterthought. But the bomb, the radiation—how had they escaped what the others hadn't? This corruption in the germ layer.

"Livia, I need to show you something."

They went up into the bedroom.

"There's a problem with mould. Damp, maybe." He removed the mirror from the wall. "See the discolouration? In fact, it's got worse."

She put her hand to where the stain had blackened like a scab. "Doesn't feel damp. If anything, it feels warm. Are there pipes running behind here?"

Ben placed his hand next to hers. "You think so?"

"We'll need to cover it before we sell the place. Paint over it, or whatever."

"Why are we whispering?"

"I don't know."

Ben looked closely at his sister. He wanted to tell her something, but she'd gone inside herself again. She wasn't coming out.

Livia was nowhere to be seen after that, so Ben was left to his own devices. There were more jobs to finish, some final cleaning and DIY. But the wrong feelings had returned.

He tried getting out again, but pacing the town he felt naked and clumsy, gawped at by pedestrians. As he crossed the shopping precinct, he saw the pregnant woman again, this time in conversation with another mother outside the post office. He skulked by the opticians and watched the pair for a while, their animated back and forth. How forced it was, he decided, this transfer of emotion through gesture, stance, eye contact. Then she saw him looking and sent a wry smile in his direction. That hastened him back inside.

Deep breath.

The house.

Expansion and contraction.

Much of the furniture had been sold or scrapped already, but the liquor cabinet was still standing. There were a few bottles left inside. He opened one and drank. Lighting one of the ancient cigarettes, he blew a plume of smoke upward and watched it spread across the ceiling. Then he took another drink. *Don't stop. Take another. Keep going until you're under the water line, down where the thoughts can't reach you.*

He went between the empty rooms, opening doors onto a dance of dust. Ray had been stripped from this place like the nitrogen scrubbed from the air. But there was something left in his wake, some strange physicality that permeated the building. What it was, he couldn't tell.

He went upstairs for another look in the mirror; the paunch and spindle legs, the borrowed clothes that didn't fit. Then it happened—a change so sudden that a bitter laugh escaped his lips.

The funhouse distortions had come upon him again—a gargantuan hand, primate elongations. And now there was movement on the inside: fluid in circulation, things in transit. But the feeling of mutation was strongest of all. Polyps, cysts, and lumps under the skin; unchecked fusions and proliferations; and tumours, tumours in organ and bone, tumours riddled with teeth and muscle and matted hair . . .

He tore the mirror from the wall and smashed it at his feet.

Deep breath.

Shards underfoot.

The wall, the bruise underneath.

Except it wasn't a bruise any longer. Now off-colour liquid seeped through the paintwork. It was a sore.

He laid his hand where some of the fluid had hardened. It was warm, just as Livia had said. Feverish warm. Again he found suppleness in place of the solid, and a deep sense of the organic emanating from the wall. *There's life here,* he realised with a kind of euphoria. And it was calling out to him.

Deep breath.

Press inward.

Lose yourself to something greater.

To be swallowed by a body so vast that imperfection was impossible. Wasn't that everything he wanted?

"I'm really losing it," he said.

He cleared away the glass, careful not to cut himself again. Then he stared at the sore a little longer. Now liquid streaked the length of the wall. Now the carpet was sodden. This was no hallucination.

"Enough."

He brought the toolbox from downstairs and rummaged inside it for a nail. The wall seemed to tense in anticipation as he held it in position. Then he drove it in with the hammer.

He tweaked the nail left and right, feeling the give of the tissue. Then he pulled it out. There was a moment where nothing happened, like the pause before pain sets in. Then the membrane shivered, and dark liquid began to bubble from the wound. It was blood—unmistakeable from the taste.

Soon the puncture had clotted. Without thinking, he pushed his finger inside to open it up again. The wall shuddered—with fear or pleasure, he didn't know. But there was no resistance on the other side. Only sap and body heat.

He removed his finger and toyed with the secretion. Then he rolled up his sleeve and squeezed his hand into the aperture. In moments he was up to his elbow in the wall. The tissue hugged him with a tingling sensation, like feeder fish on skin. It was bonding with him. Absorbing him.

Waves of contraction tugged him further in. He was afraid, but he didn't fight it. He wanted to go. Caressed by the enveloping folds, he allowed the warmth to enter him. He blinked. He closed his eyes.

Ben emerged in a film of afterbirth. He stripped down and showered, scrubbed himself until it hurt. He changed into some of his father's clothes. Then he went downstairs.

He collapsed on the living room floor. The TV was on. The news had got bored of Eyjafjallajökull. Now the headline was *Environmental Disaster in the Gulf of Mexico.* "Early reports are of an explosion at the Deepwater Horizon oil rig. As the fire rages out of control, the full extent of the spill is still unknown . . ."

Maybe he slept for a while.

After that, the house had grown cold, but he was too exhausted to do anything about it. Eventually, he managed to prop himself against the sofa. He opened his eyes. After a long period of blankness, his pupils constricted and he could see again. Livia was stood over him. "Look at you," she said. "All pink and new."

"I thought I'd gone."

"No, you're still here. Still alive."

"Yeah."

The emptiness had waned. Now his head was pounding as he tried to process what had happened upstairs. Was it a dream? Or something far worse? He pinched his nose as the pain intensified.

"Migraine?" she asked.

"Something like that."

"Here. Let me." She sat on the sofa behind him and began massaging his head. Just like when they were kids.

"Better?"

He let his head go with her hands.

"Good."

The news continued—the firestorm, the pillar of black smoke. Ben looked on in horror at the oil venting into the ocean, the expanding stain in aerial view. But he was thinking of himself. "Liv, you ever feel like you're not right . . . in your own skin, I mean?"

"All the time. It's the family disease. Just don't think about it."

"I'm trying not to."

"That's still thinking about it."

The sound of the news seemed to fade away. Then it was just the two of them.

"What was he trying to tell you?" Ben asked. "At the end?"

"Dad? Hard to say. His lungs would swallow up the words, so you had to finish the thought for him, or carry on the conversation in your head. But he did talk about the bomb."

She upped the pressure, kneading his head like dough. "Too hard," he told her. But she wasn't listening. She'd retreated inside again—the inner self hiding from the outer. Something else was speaking for her now.

"After the first test, the sky changed colour. It stayed that way for days, because of all the ash in the air. Then the colour faded, and they all started to relax. But there was radioactivity everywhere. In the rain-water they collected to drink. In the crabs they found on the beach. In the fish that bobbed to the surface of the lagoon. Those made easy suppers for the cooks on the island, so everyone ate them—seamen and officer alike. And they all got sick. Or if not them, their children."

She pressed harder, bearing down onto his scalp. "Livia, that's enough."

"But none of it really matters in the end. None of us will be spared. Because the human body is a wrong thing, isn't it? Badly organised. Easily broken. Liable to strange growths, fibroids and cancer, the mucus and slime of malfunction. I know you feel the same. Dad did too. Only he couldn't articulate it."

"I said that's enough," said Ben as he writhed on the floor. But he couldn't get away. Something was happening to the both of them.

"All these contortions needed to communicate," she said through gritted teeth. "But the deeper thoughts must find release. Or else they leak from the body and seep into reality. You've seen it. You know what I mean."

"No."

"Yes. Just look."

And she was right. He saw their reflections on the screen. Where their skin moved like ripples on water. Where their bodies merged and separated. This wasn't a trick of the light. This was really happening.

"Do you see?"

"Livia!"

"Deep breath."

"Livia, don't!"

She sighed. "But your skull is so *soft* . . ."

And with one final exertion, she pressed her fingers into him. She was in his brain. She was in his body. She was in his imperfections. And he started to cry.

AUTHOR'S NOTE

This story was inspired by eyewitness accounts of nuclear testing recalled by the author's family. The title, and some additional research, is attributable to testimony in Richard Stott's special report *The Damned: The human fallout of Britain's nuclear bombs,* available at https://damned.mirror.co.uk/

COFFIN TEXTS

RICHARD STRACHAN

AFTER SHE'S DEAD, she has so many new impressions; she's alive with them. The feel of wood makes her feel sick. The cotton of her clothes is a foul scouring. The wind in her hair puts a stone in her gut.

She craves the consistency of plastic, of cold materials that give no conversation.

She leaves work, the streets melting into the sudden wash of rain. The bus rides the hill to home. She looks down at her crossed hands in her lap, the wedding ring, the bitten nails. They pass by crowds of people who are still alive, all moving with an easy confidence through the world, tasting it, feeling it. She looks carefully at the other passengers. Are any of them dead? It's so hard to tell.

She feels like a map of visible signs, all of them pointing towards the land of the dead where she now lives.

The bus shudders, pulls out from another stop, moves on.

She can't pinpoint the exact moment. It was like the slow acknowledgement that you've abandoned an old ambition or a childhood dream. It was sad and bittersweet. It crept up on her, unassuming and polite—and then suddenly it was there.

At home, her daughter runs up to cup her legs, chattering. She arranges her face, looks at these people who might still see what they would have seen yesterday or this morning. Then the girl starts crying. She covers her face and backs away, running to her father.

What's wrong? the husband says.

He sees her then, his wife standing in the hall, her hands tightly clasped. She still has her coat on, her bag. The husband's face is blanched of emotion; then a sick expression comes creeping over it. He starts crying too. The girl howls and runs to her bedroom.

He takes his wife in his arms and buries his head in her dead hair. She can feel his tears wetting her dead neck, smell the salt in them, the lingering scents from whatever it was he was cooking.

My god, my god, he moans. I'm so sorry, so sorry ... What am I going to do!

She remembers waking once, years ago, on a day that was lit by strange storms. The light was flattened somehow, the air buoyant with ozone, sharp as steel. The husband was beside her; the girl was brewing in her womb. And at that moment, with the squirm and quiver of life in her stomach, feeling the air shift and percolate into the breaking rain, the mad profusion of it all had thrilled her. Life was absolutely intoxicating. She was drunk on what was still to come. From the bed she'd draped herself in the husband's shirt to stand at the window, looking out there at the lashed pavements, the parading rain. Such fury in it.

She thinks of this now as he cries against her shoulder. She wonders at what point does the love you feel for someone soften into habit. But she's dead now. It doesn't make any difference either way.

She cups his head in her dead hands, and with dead breath whispers soft endearments that she no longer means.

At dinner they sit in awkward silence. He's drinking heavily, swigging wine, refilling the glass, pushing his damp hair from his forehead. He glares at her, and whenever she meets his eye he looks away. Their daughter drags her spoon through the soup, sobbing quietly and snuffling.

She tries to make conversation about her day, but nothing significant comes to her. That was her last day in the world of work. She should have marked it in some way, a celebration, a mourning ritual. She will never go there again, she decides. Work is dead to her.

We can get through this, the husband says with finality, as if at the end of a conversation they haven't yet had. He clinks his glass against his plate. He frames his hands around the issue in front of them.

There's no reason we can't somehow adjust to this, find ways around it, or … We can accommodate it somehow. I know we can.

She doesn't reply. The food lies untouched in front of her, cooling on the plate. The greasy red lens of the wine in her glass trembles as he pushes up from the table. At some point their daughter has slipped from her chair and disappeared back to her bedroom, but she didn't notice.

Tomorrow, she says, but the thought drifts away from her. She looks into his eyes, numbly surprised for a moment at his interest in her.

Climbing the stairs, the feel of the banister against her hand, its polished wood, the way the smoothed grain still holds hints of its early texture. It sours her stomach. Lying down on the bed, she carefully descends to sheets that feel caustic where they touch her skin. She feels like an exposed nerve, whipping through an unfiltered world.

Rain casts coins against the window. The sound sends her into a facsimile of sleep. Lying there with her eyes open, seeing nothing, she listens to the patient tread of the husband along the corridors, to the kitchen, the back door. The smell rises up to her, the rank fragrance of things growing in the garden, buffeted by rain. The husband sighs, sobs once. What can he be thinking about? She frames herself in his thoughts for a moment, imagining what his wife must have looked like standing there in the hall; like a shadow, a shade, the half-remembered idea of the person he once knew. A vessel emptied of its contents.

To be a memory is to take up more space inside the people you love than you did when you were alive. It's the gift you give them, the other side of the exchange. He will know more of her now than he ever did before.

In the morning, descending the staircase, she announces that she'll take their daughter out for the day.

What about school, the husband says. His face is crumpled and worn, like a tissue at the bottom of a handbag. He hasn't slept all night. He watches her with cautious attention, his arms folded across his chest. He can't look at her properly. It occurs to her that she hasn't once looked at herself in a mirror since she died. She has no idea what cold casts might be forming in her eyes, the milk-white pupils clouding over, the sclera streaked with crimson fire. She raises a hand to touch the skin of her face but nothing comes away. She's still intact, still comprehensively here.

I'll take her to the museum. She used to love that. It'll be educational. It'll be better than school.

Are you sure you can manage …?

Of course. She should spend time with me. Before I'm gone. I want to spend time with her.

This feels essential all of a sudden, although the idea had only occurred to her as she approached the bottom step.

He shifts his weight from one foot to the other.

What shall I do?

She moves to answer but the words fade on her tongue, a forgotten taste.

Shielded by the kitchen door, their daughter watches, wary.

The museum is a regular haunt, but as they approach the doors it feels somehow different to her, sheathed in a caul of distance. It's near her workplace—her former workplace—and these are familiar streets, but a day into her death and everything seems subtly transformed. It's like visiting a town where you used to live after a few years' absence; all the details have been elusively rearranged. The memory fits crookedly into the gap of what you once knew.

She holds her daughter's hand and the girl doesn't complain. Her thin, squirming fingers, the heat of her skin.

Their footsteps linger against the marble, the proud atrium booming with a dozen languages. Tourists hustle in groups between the displays, pausing to snap the Burmese Buddha on his jade plinth, the racks of Polynesian cudgels and scythes. The girl untangles her fingers and rushes to the stuffed animals, gazing in wonder at the beasts, their arranged skin. The dusty giraffe stretching to the upper balconies, the rhinoceros with his fibreglass horn. Dead creatures that have lost all semblance of their former life, smoothed out now to ornament and exhibition.

Upstairs they find the Egyptian room, made mysterious by its shrouded light. Low glass cases display funerary ware, necklaces of jade and amber, scarabs in polished jet. In a sarcophagus imprinted with yellow hieroglyphs, Iufenamun the priest lies at his eternal rest. The mouldering linen of his grave wrappings mask the desiccated corpse. Amun-Ra and Hathor guard him, Isis and Osiris, the deities of his ancient worship. She imagines Iufenamun as he was back then, three thousand years ago, carrying the censer and the aspergillum, head wreathed in fragrant smoke, sandals scraping on the sandstone floor of the temple's inner precinct. Torch flames shivering in the holy silence, and the gold leaf shining flatly from the gilded statues of the gods. She presses her hands to the glass and stares down. She gazes through vertiginous time, across the millennia.

The girl seems restless, apprehensive. She flits between the cases, looking briefly at the urns and cracked jars, the beads and jewellery, avoiding the burial goods. She can't look at Iufenamun, even safely wrapped as he is, not a hint of his time-blackened skin showing.

Do they frighten you? she asks. The girls nods. Do I frighten you? The girl shakes her head. Why not?

She reaches out and touches her dead mother, cautiously, as if unsure that her fingers will connect with solid flesh.

Because you're still here, the girls says.

And he's not? She points at Iufenamun.

No, her daughter says. He's gone. He's far away.

She looks at the priest through the glass. The sarcophagus isn't a coffin, she thinks, but a ship. He's sailing, that's all; sailing into time, striking a firm course across the skin of the infinite. He's no more than a distant point on a far horizon.

Afterwards, she watches the girl wolf down a cake and drink a carton of orange juice in the cafe. Her coffee sits there cooling and untouched in front of her. The smells of soup and bread in the air seem thin and cold things, the ghosts of old plenty, half-remembered. The girl sucks at her fingers, bright tongue darting to the haphazard crumbs, her mouth ringed with chocolate. She kicks her legs beneath the chair, too short to reach the ground.

Do you like the museum?

The girl nods her head.

I wonder how many times you'll come here in your life.

Lots, the girl says. Every week. I love it.

Maybe. And every week you'll be different, won't you? You'll have grown up just that little bit more. One day, you'll be so grown up that all this will seem like a dream.

She reaches for something on the very edge of her mind, its shape indistinct. It sits there smeared in the haze of memory, uncertain.

When you're older, she tells her, you'll find …

What?

You'll find … I remember, when I was younger, there were all these moments …

She struggles for the words, for the thoughts they'll frame. Like the smells in the air that she knows should be warm and rich, the thoughts break apart the closer she gets to them. They become sad, congealed things.

Moments that would only become clear after you'd passed them, she says. And the trick is somehow *seeing* those moments as they happen, when you are in the middle of them, and knowing what they mean, knowing that the moment only happens once, before it's gone.

The girl isn't really listening. She toys with the crumbs on her plate, the crushed carton. She kicks her legs and stares around her at the long corridor of the cafe, the mezzanine floor beyond its arched doors, the high ceilings and the clustered grapes in the alabaster cornices.

She leaves her brackish coffee in its cup. She touches her hand to her face and it is cold, so cold.

They stand at the gate, by the short path to the front door. The girl's father is waiting inside, the husband. She watches the girl falter up the path, take the steps and knock. The husband's silhouette moves from the curtained window. She thinks of Iufenamun then, clasped in his grave wrappings, delivered on the tides of time into eternity.

Time, she whispers to the girl. That's all I mean. You are time made visible to me.

She turns to leave, striding carefully into the remainder of her death, leaving part of herself behind in the womb of the daughter's memory, waiting to be born. She'll be formed somewhere deep inside of her, the mother in the child.

THE INVITATION

MEGAN TAYLOR

NOT LONG AFTER Min had left the village, the world began to slip away. The distant woods were the first to go, and then the sprawling, silver-frosted fields. There was no trace of their scattered sheep or wriggling stone walls, and though she'd picked up her pace, the crest of the hill ahead of Min had vanished, everything swallowed by the mist.

She could feel it seeping inside her too. The cold was gnawing at her empty stomach, and her breath was remade before it left her mouth, but the frozen track underneath her boots kept rising, and according to Cami's directions, her parents' farm lay just over the ridge. Surely, Min would reach it soon.

Except what if there was no other side? What if her next step plunged her into nothingness—

And with the thought, she stumbled, tripping over some invisible rock or root, as if she'd cursed herself. Her arms flailed, the rucksack thumped against her back, and then the rutted ground was hurtling towards her, willing her to disappear.

Yet somehow—Min had no idea how—she managed to regain her balance. But though she remained on her feet, skin and bones intact, her heart went on juddering, and her mind was reeling, unable to catch up.

What the fuck did she think she was doing out here? When she'd told her friends about the invitation, they'd all warned her. It was too soon, they'd said, she was too desperate… And Min found herself blinking back a sheen of tears. She couldn't remember the last time that she'd felt this childishly alone, or so hopelessly, helplessly lost.

But as she fumbled to readjust her backpack's straps, Min realised that she was neither. There were soft gold spots of light floating through the milky air below her, and much nearer, only metres away, a man was drifting towards her. Perhaps Cami had sent him out to fetch her? Min's saviour, after all…

But with the mist, the man came and went. A frail, grey, flickering figure, who suddenly appeared child-sized and more lost than Min. For a moment, his sadness seemed tangible—the clouds between them grew colder and damper—and as he faded in and out, she wondered if, like her, he'd floundered. It was hard to tell, but he might have been down on his knees, and scrambling, and "Hello?" she called out. "Do you need help?"

But of course, the mist muffled her voice; she tried again. "Hello? *Hello?*"

He bleated in response.

"For fuck's sake," Min muttered, attempting to smile. As weird and white as the universe had become, she couldn't understand how she'd managed to mistake a sheep for a man, or even a boy. She began to move towards its hazy, stunted shape, but it was already floating away, carried off by the tide along with everything else—everything except for those gentle holes of light, which could only be windows—farmhouse windows. Ignoring the untrustworthy ground and clinging cold, Min broke into a run.

The house emerged like a ghost-ship. Its stone walls were so pallid they were edgeless, but Min was able to make out a long, dark, prow-like roof and the suggestion of chimneys. And while she couldn't see the woodsmoke, as its scent wafted over her, she could feel how close Cami was—that new, sharp thrill was back, thawing her freezing gut—and gazing at those gilded panes, she knew that she'd been right to come. Greedily, she breathed the woodsmoke in.

And now, the farmhouse door was opening, spilling out more gold light and the richer, unmistakable tang of roasting meat, and despite her recent switch from veggie to full-on vegan, Min's mouth was watering. She couldn't wait to get inside.

Inside was another world. When Min had entered the kitchen, she'd been hit by the heat, and only the air above the stove was blurred with steam; the rest of the room was shining. A deep, reddish glow danced between the coppery pots and the cupboards and the countertops, and the eyes of the women circling Min were gleaming too, alive with firelight.

From her seat at the polished oak table, Min was doing her best to keep her gaze on the crackling hearth. Trying to keep track of the twisting flames felt easier than looking directly at Cami's mother or her sister, or even at Cami. The last time that Min glanced over, Cami had been hovering over the pots, the tantalisingly rosy tip of her tongue caught between her even, glinting teeth.

The family resemblance was startling. While Cami's sister was slightly rounder and her mother obviously an older version, they had the same thick, dark, silky curls and impeccable, creamy complexions. Their mouths were firm and full and painted boldly crimson, and the fact that they shared a taste in lipstick was somehow more unnerving than their similar smiles. There was too much beauty in the room.

"You must be starving," Cami's mother said, "after coming so far. All those trains and buses, I can't imagine. But I'm afraid that dinner isn't quite ready… Perhaps this will fill a hole?"

She placed a small, clay bowl on the table, forcing Min to look up, but as soon as Min met those familiar, smouldering eyes, she found herself blinking away again, and blushing. Only her grumbling stomach didn't care.

Without thinking, she'd reached for the bowl, and she was on the verge of digging in before she realised what it held.

Scratchings, she suspected, taking in the bronzed, misshapen morsels, with their crisp, curled edges and tiny, glistening blisters, their sweetly greasy, festive scent. The smell was nearly as instinctively, dirtily tempting as whatever meat was painstakingly roasting, and for a few bewildering seconds, Min considered giving in.

Instead, she knotted her hands together in her lap. She hadn't eaten meat in seven years, and she couldn't work out where the impulse had come from. Perhaps it was something to do with the countryside air—the mist that was still filling the windows—or maybe it was simply down to her nerves, a cowardly urge to appear polite. For the first time in a long time, it felt awkward trying to explain.

"I'm sorry," she began. "I don't... I can't..."

And both Cami's mother and sister began to laugh, a low but distinctive husky laugh, which was exactly how Cami had reacted when Min had first mentioned going vegan. Although they'd met on an environmental march, Cami seemed incapable of taking Min's choices seriously. *My little lentil-head,* she'd said.

But wasn't Cami's playfulness part of her charm? Combined with her easy confidence and those undeniable looks, it was no wonder that Min had fallen so hard, so fast. She couldn't understand why her friends refused to understand. Yes, it had been a whirlwind—she'd known Cami less than a month—but there wasn't any need for their concern.

"You're already meeting the family?" Jon had spluttered. "You're not thinking straight, Min, you're love-drunk. It'll only end in tears."

But Jon had always had a jealous streak, and he hadn't had a new girlfriend in over six months. He probably imagined that Min and Cami were at it like rabbits; no one could deny their chemistry...

"Such self-restraint," Cami's mother murmured. But she was pushing the bowl closer, and then jiggling it, exposing the scratchings' golden undersides and a tiny gathering pool of amber-coloured juice.

"Mother!" Cami's sister had turned from the drawer where she'd been rummaging. "There's nothing wrong with a bit of restraint." She was clutching a knife, and as she spoke, its curved blade flashed. "If our guest wants to save herself for later, then you need to leave her be."

Min's blush returned, renewed, but though her skin was burning, she leant back towards the fire, trying to lose herself once more in its flickering shapes. She didn't think it would work, but within seconds, the flames became a radiant forest, full of writhing trees, and then the branches parted, and staring harder, she glimpsed a molten wolf, with a stretching jaw. She watched its long, gold tongue reel out...

But she was abruptly aware of Cami's gaze licking over her too, and there was no distracting herself from the sudden desire that rippled through her in response. Since Cami had first grabbed her at that march, she'd had the power to make Min's body ache. There had been so many occasions, like this, when even Min's bones seemed to squirm with wanting. She felt melded to her seat.

And yet, so far, despite what Jon imagined, they hadn't gone much further than kissing, and a little touching. But oh, those kisses, those touches…

"Wine?"

With a start, Min realised that Cami was standing right behind her, holding a brimming glass of red, and without asking about its origins or ingredients, Min nodded mutely, just as she had when Cami had proposed this visit to her family home. The invitation was a no-brainer—the opportunity to spend a night, bound together, with Cami, in her childhood bed—how could Min say no?

And she was as thirsty, she realised, as she was hungry, and though the wine was thick and tart, so full-bodied it bordered on aggressive, it coated her mouth with warmth, and before Min knew it, she'd emptied the glass. It had slipped down so easily.

Cami or her sister or her mother, or all three of them, started to laugh again, that same throaty, carefree laugh, and mortified, Min turned back to the flames, and the wolf was leaping now. And as it pounced, it transformed into an angel or a devil-woman, with streaming wings or spreadeagled limbs, and behind Min, the laughter changed, the women muttering among themselves

But although their husky voices were hushed, "Why don't you give her the tour," Min overheard the mother suggest. "The hunger will drive her crazy if we keep her waiting here."

The shadows in the hallway were so soft they might have been gas-lit, and while Cami flitted ahead, Min found herself having to concentrate on each shuffling step. But maybe that was the wine as much as the dusky, little wall lamps? Min's face felt heavy, suffused with too much sluggish blood, and the passage seemed to be curving in on her, although it was far longer than she'd expected.

It was impossible to gauge the building's size, and while Min had hoped that the 'tour' might involve Cami showing her their room—for the hundredth time, Min imagined tangling with Cami under the quaintly pastoral folds of a patchwork quilt—so far, Cami hadn't paused at any of the dim, closed doors they'd passed. And nor was she distracted by the photographs, which cluttered the walls between the doors, a family gallery that did nothing to stop Min dragging her feet.

Most of the pictures were of laughing little girls with creamy cheeks and wild, dark hair and dancing eyes, and though Min squinted, she couldn't distinguish Cami from her sister, or even her mother. The timeless smocked dresses and tricycles and ponies didn't help, and it was almost a relief when the portraits changed, all that relentless prettiness giving way to two awkward, gangling boys.

Min had forgotten about Cami's younger brothers, but as she peered at the teenagers' stiff, old-fashioned blazers and hunted-looking eyes, she recalled Cami mentioning boarding school. "Best place for them," she'd said. "We've got to let them have their chance."

But the boys hardly exuded a sense of opportunity. Their smiles looked strained and strangely aged, and they were so skinny, they might have been malnourished. It hardly seemed possible that they shared Cami's blood, but perhaps they'd inherited their father's looks?

And belatedly remembering the other man in Cami's life, Min called out to her, "When am I going to meet your dad?"

Cami didn't turn back. Having made it, at last, to the hallway's end, she was busy heaving at the bolts, Min saw, of a looming back door, and when she answered, her voice was interrupted by a series of hollow clanks.

"Maybe, later… He isn't… Well…"

And just before the final bolt scraped free, Min heard something else. A wheedling cry came creeping out from behind the nearest closed door, and as the sound built and then broke open, becoming high-pitched sobs, Min's empty stomach lurched with pity.

"How sick is he?" she mumbled.

But Cami's laughter drowned out the noise, and "The baby," she was saying, "my niece… She's always hungry!", and then she was shouting past Min, towards the kitchen—"*Awake,*" she yelled—and at the same time, the heavy back door gave way, and the passageway stiffened, bristling with the misty chill.

Min shivered, standing in front of the barn's giant, black mouth. "Maybe," she suggested, "we'd be better off doing this in the morning?"

But Cami had produced a torch from somewhere, and "Maybe not," she replied, clicking it on. Her graceful, capable hands reappeared in a brief, flaring burst of gold, and as she lifted the beam, Min caught a glimpse of her elegant throat and her full, soft, curving lips.

"I think that tonight is perfect."

Min did her best to return Cami's smile, but the mist was also weaving through the torchlight, and as Cami strode into the barn, it rolled after her like magicians' smoke, and afraid of being left off-stage, Min hurried to catch up.

She'd hoped that with the evening coming in, the mist would have started to thin, but only the shadows in the barn had managed to hold it at bay, and they didn't feel like a reprieve. They were so solid, the torch's glow could barely touch them, and the smells that came bowling over Min were just as dense. A swampy combination of slick, dank fur, and mouldering compost, and rotting wood... Breathing shallowly though her mouth, Min had never felt so much like a city girl, but as if Cami had read her mind, she called out through the dark.

"Don't be scared, my Min! I only want to keep you safe. There's no need to panic."

And with her voice, the torchlight swung upwards, illuminating scorched-looking rafters and a row of glinting hooks, and then, as it descended, bales of straw like matted hair, and two shining yellow eyes—

But before Min could take in that glare, the shadows erupted, flapping towards her, and she was staggering backwards, about to turn and run. But her boots stuck in something thick and wet, and then Cami was right there, beside her, and "Chickens," she was murmuring, the word warm against Min's ear.

"Oh!" Min said, and then more quietly, "Oh..."

And as Cami drew the beam across the wide, dirt floor, calmly picking out several strutting, downy shapes, Min tried to laugh. But her giggles sounded fake, and when she spoke, she could only whisper. "I thought you might have bats."

With her spare hand, Cami squeezed Min's shoulder. "Wouldn't that have been good?" she said. "But sadly, no. There's just the Sussex Fowls in here, and of course, this is where we keep our dear old nanny too."

"Your *nanny*?"

For a moment, Min pictured an old woman hobbling between the barn's black corners, her once-silky hair curling into the shadows, her skin glimmering like sour cream. Instead, as Cami redirected the torch, those yellow eyes returned.

And as they grew clearer—surprisingly lushly lashed, and so wide-set they appeared bolted onto each side of the long-muzzled skull—Min released a genuine laugh. It was the second time today that she'd been fooled by a farmyard animal. The goat gazed back at her, unfazed.

She was a moth-eaten, misshapen creature. Although her stomach hung low and bloated, her legs were spindly, and Min could practically count her ribs, and that bony face didn't look right either. Her mouth appeared too large for her head, and she was chewing with such intensity that her jaw seemed about to come unhinged.

"Cami," Min said, still whispering. "Don't you think that we ought to get back to the house? Dinner might be ready by now, and I don't want to look rude…"

"Always thinking with your gut!" Cami exclaimed, but she sounded delighted, and as she closed in, surrounding Min with her delicious warmth, Min found herself imagining that fantasy bedroom again. She thought about lying naked among those patchwork folds, with Cami's mouth on her throat… And forgetting the shadows and the smells and the watching goat, she reached out for Cami in return, craving her perfect lips.

But the goat hadn't forgotten them. Before they could kiss, the nanny was barging into their thighs, nudging Cami away, and Min heard the rhythmic *chomp-chomp-chomp* of that endlessly grinding, oversized mouth. But when Cami lowered the torch, she saw that the goat's chewing head was bowed to the dirt. And then Min saw what she was grazing on—

"What the fuck?" Min cried, flinching backwards, her boots not sticking now, but skidding.

The ground was strewn with feathers and blood and lumps of raw, stringy meat, but rather than whipping the beam away, Cami swept it slowly on, until it settled on a beak, flapping skin, and a severed neck, trailing what might have been tendons.

"Looks like the new rooster's had it," she said. "That's the second one this month."

Back in the kitchen, despite the fire's blaze, Min couldn't stop trembling. What she'd seen in the barn had been sickening—she couldn't stop seeing it—and as if the goat hadn't been bad enough, just before Min had stumbled out, the chickens had gathered around the nanny's cloven hooves. She'd glimpsed them pecking, eating too.

But Cami didn't seem in the least perturbed. When they'd returned to the house, she hadn't mentioned what had happened to the rooster, or his remains. She'd slipped so smoothly back into her family's warmth, as if nothing was wrong, but perhaps she was simply trying to preserve the peace. The kitchen was such a contrast to the barn's darkness and cold and inhuman brutality, a scene of domestic bliss...

Sitting next to Min at the table, Cami's sister was nursing the baby. Head gently bowed, her dark curls merged with her daughter's surprisingly thick, matching hatch, and every now and then, a pale, pretty, little starfish-hand escaped the bundled blankets, and then the baby would burrow deeper, resuming her determined grip.

Meanwhile, Cami's mother was gliding between the dresser and the table, setting out plates and silverware. Dinner was clearly about to be served, but after what Min had witnessed, she didn't know if she could face it. The waves of nausea hadn't fully subsided. Her throat remained half-closed, and her tongue felt tainted, her saliva as thick as grease.

"More wine?" Cami offered.

After presenting Min with another generous glass, she joined her mother, who'd returned to the stove, and while Min managed a tentative sip, they worked together, swapping pan lids and spoons and last-minute seasonings. It was the first time that Cami had cooked for Min, but though her culinary skills appeared as artful as everything else that she did, they didn't do anything to ease Min's anxiety. After all this effort, she couldn't imagine making excuses. She'd have to force herself to eat.

But in her head, the goat went on chewing, and the chickens pecked, and as Cami lifted a dribbling ladle to her red, wet mouth, Min's stomach squeezed and shuddered, and she broke into a prickling sweat. But then, still sucking eagerly on the ladle's loaded bowl, Cami caught Min's eye, and her nausea transformed.

A different kind of feverish heat rippled over Min as her longing returned. Where a second ago, her guts had been swilling, she felt that sweetly painful, quivering ache, and then the sensation was building and spreading. Every inch of her skin was tingling, yearning to be touched, and suddenly nothing mattered except Cami's stove-hot hands, and her dripping mouth—

Beside Min, Cami's sister gasped.

Flustered, Min turned to her, only to find her head thrown back, her spine arching against her chair. She was lifting the baby away from her like an offering, seemingly unaware that she'd left her breasts exposed.

Min turned away quickly. She stared into her glass, and then lifted it, and as the wine washed over her tongue, she shut her eyes. But now, instead of the goat and its meal, she was helplessly picturing Cami's sister's flesh.

Her breasts were beautiful, full and perfectly rounded. Their smooth, pale skin was tenderly marked with tiny pink smudges, like a trail of fingerprints.

"Little biter," Cami's sister muttered.

But when Min opened her eyes, careful to look only at Cami's sister's face, she was gazing at her baby with affection, and "She's cutting her first tooth", she explained, her voice glowing with pride.

"She's eager," Cami's mother agreed, slamming the oven door, and turning from the range. "She can't wait to eat her meat."

And then, abruptly, there it was. Before Min could prepare herself, Cami and her mother were covering the table with dishes piled high with cutlets and crackling. There were platters of steak-like strips, and fat, pallid fillets, and bowls crammed with what looked like tartare and something liverish, and as Min's gaze passed over what might have been home-made cocktail sausages bobbing in a dish of purplish jus, she felt dazzled. There wasn't a vegetable in sight.

"Um," Min tried to begin. "I thought you knew…"

But the women were ignoring her. Cami's mother was wielding a massive roasting tin, and as she set it down with a flourish, they released a collective sigh.

The aroma rolled over Min along with their exhaled breath. A heady, musky barbecue scent, it had a coppery edge to its sweetness that made Min wonder if it was pork, or possibly veal; it was hard to tell. It was darkly charred, and an odd, elongated shape. Maybe it was beef, or venison? Or goat—*for fuck's sake, please not goat—*

"Shall I do the honours?" Cami asked.

She was standing over the meat, holding an oversized, long-pronged fork and a carving knife, and beaming. But Min couldn't take in her smile anymore; she was panicking. The baby, who'd nestled back against her mother, paused her guzzling to loudly smack her lips, and Cami's mother was leaning across the heaving table, reaching for Min's plate.

"Please," Min blurted, "*wait.*"

And all three of them—no, four; the baby had also turned her wobbling, well-fed head—were looking at Min. Regarding her with the same wide, dark, playful eyes, and their shared amusement made Min feel thinned, about to disappear once more.

"I…I…" she stuttered. "I thought…" In desperation, she tried to appeal just to Cami. "I thought your dad might be joining us?"

She wasn't sure where the notion had come from, but as a delaying tactic, if nothing else, it seemed momentarily inspired.

Except Cami didn't reply. Instead, without breaking her stare, she plunged her fork into the roast, and her sister gulped back a giggle.

But Cami's mother was frowning. "Now, now, girls," she said, "be kind. Look how kind our guest is, to be worrying." And then, addressing Min, "I'm afraid that my husband is confined to his room, for the most part."

"Oh," Min said. "Well, in that case, would you like me to take him his dinner? I could introduce myself…"

And though she was still simply buying time, the idea felt more than inspiring; it seemed like a gift. Cami's mother was no longer staring at Min but glancing past her to the mist at the window.

"Hmmm," she said. "What a charitable thought… I never like him to feel neglected."

Min jumped to her feet. "Please go ahead," she said, "and start without me."

But when she glanced at Cami, Cami didn't look happy. She dropped the knife with a clatter and stepped reluctantly away from the meat. But then Cami's mother caught hold of her wrist.

"It's okay, Darling," she soothed. "Your little friend will be fine if we let her go alone. I'm sure she'll hurry back."

Outside, in the passage again, Min loitered uncertainly in front of the third closed door. Although the tray was heavy, and Cami's mother had been specific in her directions, Min wasn't convinced that she'd found the right room. Wasn't this where the crying had come from? Had she been sent to the nursery?

Still fretting, she shifted the tray and knocked, but while she waited for a reply that she somehow knew wasn't going to come, she became increasingly aware of the boys in the pictures, huddled around her. They seemed to be watching her, beseeching her, with their despairing, underfed eyes, and when she couldn't take the pressure of their tragic gazes any longer, she reached out clumsily for the handle, and forced herself inside.

"Incoming!" she called, attempting to sound light-hearted, but her warning quavered out of her, and as she stumbled over the threshold, Min nearly dropped the tray.

The room was dimly lit, and freezing, and its shivering shadows reeked. It smelt more like the barn than the house; there was a similar animal fustiness, the same underlying rot.

In comparison, the steam rising from the tray smelt heartening, and disregarding the dishes' contents, Min bowed her head, breathing in the fumes instinctively before she looked around. Her vision was struggling to adjust.

The only light came from a small, flickering lamp, set next to the darkly heaped bed, and a narrow window. But the window's gleam didn't make much sense. Outside, the night would have deepened, and yet the mist was glowing more brightly than ever, and Min wondered if it was some sort of weird natural phenomena, like will-o-the-wisps, or phosphorescent algae... But then the bedsprings whinged, interrupting her thoughts. The lumpen shadows stirred.

She swallowed hard, and then "Hello," she began, walking over. "I'm Min. I'm Cami's friend. She invited me out here for the night. She wanted me to see the farm, and meet you all, and everybody's been so welcoming. They've been cooking up a storm."

Already, Min worried, she'd started to babble, but as she approached the bed, her voice trailed off. "I didn't want you to miss out..."

The man wasn't lying down, like she'd expected. As his narrow frame emerged, she saw the crush of pillows that had been used to prop him into sitting up, but he didn't look comfortable. Although Min couldn't make out his expression in the lamp's weak flutter, there was something distinctly pained-looking about the angle of his neck.

In fact, everything about his posture looked painful. Despite the abundant pillows, his body was covered, from chin to toe, in just a single, flimsy sheet, and though his proportions seemed off in a way that Min couldn't fully grasp, she could clearly see how cold he was. The cotton was vibrating with his shivering, and newly aware of the icy air slicing through her too, Min glanced back to the window, and, yes, it had been left ajar.

And surprising herself, Min sprang into action, dumping the tray on the floor, and then bounding across the room to slam the casement shut. She couldn't believe anyone could have been so careless, the man was so obviously suffering; it felt almost deliberately cruel... And as Min fumbled to fasten the catch, the mist banked up against the panes went on glowing—*gloating,* she thought—and shaking her head, she turned her back on it. But it hadn't quite left the room.

Silvery threads spun delicately among the darkness, and a thicker, cobwebby veil hung over the bed, draping that poor, cold man, and for a few confusing seconds, it appeared to be gusting out of him, but that wasn't what made Min shudder. As she stared into the haze, she recalled the sheep that she'd seen, or almost seen, on the track outside, and the sadness that had swirled over her, that palpable sense of loss...

Cami's father seemed to be emanating the same sorrowful waves, and as Min waded through them, back towards the bed, *he's so alone,* she found herself thinking, *and empty. But aren't we all, at heart, lonely and empty? Desperate, and hollowed-out...*

But by the time she'd reached his side, the thought was gone, and the illusion had faded. There weren't any gossamer clouds left clinging to the chilly air, just the dingy shadows crowding in.

Still, "Are you okay?" Min asked stupidly, leaning close, and then reaching out to angle the lamp to see him properly.

He recoiled from the light, and Min stepped back, wincing too. He looked so weak and vulnerable, and far too old to be Cami's father, or even her grandfather. His skin, stretched like worn, grey silk across his long, gaunt face, barely covered his skull, but his eyes, although sunken and colourless, appeared alert, and he was trying to lift his chin, possibly to study Min in turn, and she picked up the tray to show him the bowls. Maybe he hadn't understood?

But when she glanced back, his mouth had dropped open, revealing a white-furred, wormy tongue, and bloodless gums, pocked with sore-looking gaps instead of teeth, and how, she wondered, would he manage to eat? She might need to mash up the meat or feed him the juice like soup. She desperately wanted to offer him something, to help somehow. She'd never smelt breath so rancid.

But perhaps it wasn't his mouth that stank. As Min pushed aside the pillows, attempting to balance the tray on his shaky lap, she inadvertently dragged the sheet free too, exposing his body, or what remained of it. Cami's father wasn't whole.

His left arm was missing entirely, and the right ended where an elbow should have been. Both stumps had been roughly packed with wadded gauze, and there were more bandages clinging to his bare, mottled chest. The wounds were clearly weeping; the dressings were sallow with damp, and the waistband of his pyjama bottoms was glistening stickily, and as Min's stunned gaze dipped lower, she saw that only one of his pyjama-legs appeared to be in use; the other sagged with a sickening looseness over the mattress's edge.

"Fuck," Min gasped. She could hardly catch her breath. "Oh, what the fuck..."

Why hadn't Cami warned her? Why hadn't any of those sleek,

laughing women explained what had happened to mutilate this pitiful man? Had he been the victim of some horrific farm accident, or was it one of those freaky flesh-eating diseases…

Min glanced back to the man's chest, but not at his dressings. Although the skin around his bandages was unbroken, it was scattered with small bruises. The blotches reminded Min of the tiny suck-marks on Cami's sister's breasts, except that these were far more numerous, and here and there, they ran together. They merged to form a particularly livid rash in the shadow of his ribs.

And for the first time, Min took in his ribcage. The jutting bones, both sharp and fragile, made her want to cry, and as she gazed between them and his shrivelled stomach, it struck her that this man wasn't just sick, he was emaciated; he was *starving*.

A sudden heat cut through the chill as Min groped for the tray, and as she drew in the rich scents from the dishes once more, she was transported back to the kitchen, with its bustling warmth, and the idea of it, here, beside this husk of a man, was mind-boggling. Were the women in there still laughing? Or had they started to eat, stuffing their red, wet, eager mouths.

But the man, peering tearfully up at her, slowly closed his mouth, concealing his ravaged gums, and though Min was abruptly busy, loading a spoon with the tenderest-looking morsels that she could find, he kept his thin lips shut.

"You must eat," she begged him. "*Please*."

The spoon overflowed as she lifted it, but Min ignored the small, dark splashes spattering his wasted chest, and pushed it closer, trying to tempt him—and how could he not be tempted?

The smell of the meat was intriguing. Tantalising and delectable, irresistible… And he badly needed sustenance, there was so little left of him, only the most meagre portions, and aware of his hunger like a gaping void, "It's delicious," Min pressed on. "Try one small taste, just a couple of bites…" She was trying to echo Cami's seductive voice, her most inviting tones. "We all need to be fed."

And suddenly, Min's hand was turning. The spoon was hovering next to her mouth, and as it kissed her lips, she could feel the anticipation flooding her own waiting stomach and beating with her blood. For a moment, the longing was pure and joyous, and then it overwhelmed her, and Min began to eat.

THE EIGHTH ROOM

ZACHARIAH CLAYPOLE WHITE

THE HOUSE HAS SEVEN ROOMS. A bedroom, bathroom, kitchen, and office clustered together on the first floor; a smaller guest bedroom and bathroom, with no shower, on the second. Across from the upstairs bedroom is another room. We have not yet decided its purpose. The house is quiet, too far from the road for more than the growl of passing semis to reach us. We do not include the basement in our count: it can only be accessed from the garden. We find the eighth room by accident.

We have never owned a house before; we catalogue every detail, proving its existence and our possession. This house has nine doors (excluding the basement), nineteen outlets mounted on eggshell walls, four windows on the top floor and eight on the bottom. After the first night, we find the bedroom window cracked in a shapeless sort of way. "It was a bird," we say, although neither of us heard the crunch of hollow bones. There is no body, feathers, or blood. The longer we stare at the jagged lines, the more we are reminded of ocean surf before a hurricane.

Three days here and still we unpack dishes. Most have survived the U-Haul. We're opening the last box when we notice the fridge is leaking. We consider calling a plumber, even scroll through Yelp reviews of local contractors, but no, this is our house, our first house. Another's hands should not be allowed inside its cupboards, its pipes, and crawl-spaces. We will fix it.

Moving the fridge is harder than we imagined, an awkward shuffle across the linoleum: a two-step with no sense of rhythm or grace. Beneath florescent light, the wall reveals itself.

There, where the fridge stood, is a room the size of a flat-rate shipping box. At first, we do not consider it a room. Perhaps it is a builder's mistake, or an alcove for a long-defunct appliance. *Yes,* we think. *Surely that.* Then we look closer.

Here is what the eighth room contains:

- A miniature bed-frame, five by six inches.
- A window, cracked in a way that seems familiar, looking into the blackness of drywall. Although, we think, *Isn't drywall white*?

We move the fridge back.

We do not sleep soundly in our new house. At night the bedroom window lets in too much light and during the day, not enough. Our sheets are the deep blue of glacial ice, our rug the color of ocean grass. On the walls we hang portraits of family, our college diplomas, the final postcard from an absent friend. For a while we find these comforting, but soon the colors are storm-ridden. Every evening the photographs seem to change—a parade of strangers slowly occupies our wall.

On the fifth day the fridge sits exactly fourteen inches into the kitchen's center. We tell each other, "I did not move it," and try not to look at the wall.

Here is what the eighth room now contains:

- A miniature bed perhaps five by six inches, with dark blue sheets.
- A window, more cracked than before.
- A tiny rug, ocean-green.
- Several rectangles hung along the walls, each half the size of a first-class stamp. They could be family photographs, certificates, posters of missing children. We do not bother counting them.

We move the fridge back.

We dream ourselves lying in a familiar bed, but the portraits are indistinct, the colors blurred—as if seen from a great distance, or viewed through a magnifying glass. The window looks out over nothing. When we wake we do not open our eyes, afraid of which room we will discover.

We find the marionettes on the eighth day. The fridge has moved again (we do not bother accusing each other this time). The hidden room is once again unhidden. And occupied. Two jointed mannequins (such as an artist might use to learn a body) are sitting on the miniature bed, looking out through the now shattered window. The dolls have no eyes, mouths, or fingers. They are white as bleach, their faces empty as a starless sky.

Tonight, all the glass falls from the bedroom window. There is no sound. The house has simply decided this window can no longer be a window. That it was never, in fact, a window. Only the impression of one: a copy. We startle awake from dreams we do not discuss and watch night pour across the windowsill. Our hands clutch the bedding but do not touch. How pale we become in the moonlight.

Here is the secret—shared but never told: there are more than eight rooms in this house. Every room holds in itself another. We hear fingerless hands sculpting fresh architecture behind the drywall.

We speak in lies. The house takes our voices, holds them in its contours, lets them trickle back to us like a dripping faucet. We open our throats to this place; exist only as language for those moving in the walls.

Today is our last. In the eighth room, unlike ours, the window has been repaired. The mannequins stand by their bed, each holding a tiny blade. The mattress between them is a flame-licked red, and the red flows down into the kitchen. We look to the counter. From the knife block, two handles are missing. We move the fridge back against the wall, a puddle thickly leaking out from beneath it.

Soon we will fix the window, and soon we will complete our house.

Slowly, almost peacefully, we return to the room.

LEMMINGS

KIRSTYN MCDERMOTT

YOU LIKELY KNOW the game by now, or at least know of it. Can picture the little dudes, with their shock of green hair and blue . . . overalls? Onesies? Athleisure wear? Who can tell from a handful of pixels? Marching in lockstep as lemmings do, right over the edge of a cliff, or into a bubbling green tank of acid, or mangled by one of the gear machines. Just a handful of pixels, though, and not a one of them ever turning red. It was a big deal, back in its day—sales and rankings and countless obsessive hours eaten up chasing the quickest time, the highest percentage, level after addictive goddamn level. But if you've played the game, it's been on an emulator, right? Appreciating the retro graphics and simplistic mechanics, shaking your head over the clunky controls and wondering how people sat still for shit like this for so long, wondering that even as it winds you in and whispers its second-hand nostalgia right into your cortex—if nostalgia can be the right word for a time you never knew. Because if you did know it, if you weren't just alive but old enough to play the game on your Commodore 64 or fledgling PC or, hell, the original Amiga version, then you're here on another mission. You're reading this for answers, or clues at the very least. You're shopping for reasons, but we're fresh out of those. (See also: toilet paper, hand sanitiser, unsullied dreams.) We don't know why. We only know what. And we knew it first.

Finally. Jinx screenshots the end-of-level infodump before carefully transcribing the next level code into her notebook, just in case. She's lost screenshots before and, besides, there's something about having all the level codes written down in her own hand that feels comforting. That feels real. Listed down the page in chunky blue capitals, it looks like Egyptian hieroglyphs or notes a Russian spy might keep. Of course, what would be even better is if she could just put a pin in her progress each session, but the game dates back from before genius programmers thought up the whole "save game" concept. Whatever. *Lemmings* is worth it, the best of the bunch of archaic video games that Tyler hooked them into back when lockdown looked like only lasting till the end of term. Three months later and Jinx has ditched them all —*Lode Runner, Prince of Persia, Archon,* a dozen others she can't even remember now—and is patiently eking out her fave at the rate of no more than one new level a day. It's a dead game, frozen in silicone, and once she's played it through, she's played it forever.

Sitting on its charger, her phone sounds the bleat of a fainting goat, the novelty alert weeks past its best-by but Jinx can't summon the effort to change it. The message is from Cazz, peppered with multiple emojis: several astonished faces, three different gravestones, and a purple cat. There's always a purple cat.

seen it yet???

Jinx thumbs a response. *seen what???*

omg!! the SUICIDE its evrywhr!!

She doesn't even have time to open TikTok before her bedroom door swings wide and there's her dad, hand outstretched, face caught somewhere between furious and terrified. Jinx remembers that look from those last days with her mum, driving home from hospice each night, her dad clutching the steering wheel so tight she expected to see indentations in the vinyl cover when he finally let go.

"Phone," he says. "Now."

Jinx rolls her eyes, trying for casual. Her stomach isn't having it, is already churning up a fresh batch of anxiety. "What, I can't even talk to my friends now?"

"That's not ... please, the phone."

She locks it before surrendering. Her dad switches the device off, shoves it into the back pocket of his jeans. When he sits down on the bed, it's right near the edge, as far from her as he can manage to keep, and the mattress sags dramatically. He wobbles, rights himself. Jinx wants to laugh, but worries she might not stop.

"It's not a punishment, Janelle." He's staring at the ground between his feet, like the manky grey carpet holds infinitely more interest than his daughter's face ever could. "Your school texted me. There's something going around the socials right now, so best if you stay off them for bit, yeah? Just till it's cleaned up."

Jinx shrugs, whatever, no big deal, like her phone isn't a lifeline of any kind. "A virus?"

"Just a video. Some sick f—person who thinks it's funny to scare kids."

"I've probably seen worse."

He does look at her then. She wishes he hadn't. It's worse than the mum-is-dying face, somehow, even though Jinx doesn't really know how to decode it with any precision. Like Jinx killed his puppy, is how she might describe it to Cazz, or maybe like Jinx is the puppy.

"You haven't been out today, right?" Her dad stands, absently reaches round to pat the phone still in his pocket. "Why don't you go for a walk, kiddo? Get some fresh air."

Fresh air wasn't something they used to worry about much, till lockdown. Now it's all *go outside* this, *get your exercise* that, sixty minutes, five kays, blah blah blah. No one she actually knows lives within five kays; she hasn't seen her friends outside of a screen since forever. Sometimes she catches herself wondering if they still exist, if they aren't just data on a server somewhere, blipping into life at her beck and call.

What if all we ever were is data, she asked Cazz a couple of weeks back. *Would we even know any different?*

The girl on the screen stared at her through a pinkish orange fringe, uneven home-colour job that didn't really take but, hey, that's what filters are for. *Keep it together, girl. Don't matrix-out on me.*

"Janelle?" Her dad snaps two fingers in front of her face. "Exercise?"

Jinx scowls. "Okay if I get dressed first?" She grabs the hem of her pyjama top, makes a show of being about to yank it over her head. Her dad flinches and flees the room, leaving the door pointedly ajar behind him. She waits until she hears him messing about in the kitchen before retrieving her old phone from where she's stashed it between the mattress and base. The thing is stone-cold dead and doesn't have a working SIM, but she finds an old cable and plugs it in beneath the desk. By the time she gets back, it'll be charged and ready to suck down some Wi-Fi.

Jinx smiles as she pulls on her shoes and grabs a clean mask. Like she wouldn't keep a spare.

In real life, lemmings are a monumental disappointment. Small arctic hamsters, or some distant cousin, brown and tailless with a penchant for extreme cliff-diving if their population gets out of control, or so you'll no doubt have heard. It's not even the weirdest notion to have attached itself to them. Lemmings spontaneously generating within storms and falling from the sky like fat, furry hailstones. Lemmings harbouring a rage so cataclysmic they eventually explode, strewing pelts and body parts all over the landscape for naïve naturalists to stumble over. But lemmings as suicide squad, blindly following one another to their collective doom—that's the story that stuck, thanks mostly to Disney. An intrepid group of documentarians on the payroll of an altogether different rodent, trudging through the arctic wilderness to capture on film the fabled mass migration of lemmings, cameras unflinching as the animals tumbled from a cliff to splash into the choppy, frigid waters of the ocean below. The filmmakers even nabbed an Academy Award. But it's all a goddamned lie. Alberta, to start with, not the Arctic circle. Inuit kids contracted to bring in the lemmings, the bounty a few pennies a piece. A giant turntable swinging those same confused creatures around again and again, that old animation background trick rejigged for close focus. And then the grand finale: herding the lemmings towards the edge, over the edge, little claws no doubt scrabbling for any kind of purchase as they realised the fatality of their error. The desperation of their fall. The terror of their end. It was never suicide; we want you to see that. It was nothing less than mass murder.

The bin at the edge of the park is overflowing. Takeaway coffee cups mostly, and some disposable masks, their thin, white elastic twisted yet intact. Jinx remembers the short clip someone shared a couple of weeks ago: those clumps of used masks on beaches, in riverbeds, clinging to grassy verges; death-traps tangled around the legs of sea birds and other critters, one even found in the belly of a dead turtle. *Be responsible,* the voiceover pleaded, *tear off the elastic before you throw your mask away!* Such a simple request, the work of less than a second, less than a thought, and yet.

For a brief, hope-thin moment back there it looked like things might be starting to change. People bringing their own coffee cups to cafes, their own bags to supermarkets. Single-use plastics on the way out, recycling on the rise. Maybe, just maybe there was a corner being turned, however slowly, however reluctantly—or smugly, depending on the type of zero-waste lifestyle you could afford to lead.

But now, one panicked whiff of pandemic, and it's all gone to shit.

Single use *everything* and all anyone's talking about is COVID, infection rates, death counts, and how soon a vaccine might be produced. No one's looking more than two steps in front of them anymore.

Jinx remembers the climate protests last year, marching elbow to elbow with Cazz as they brandished their hand-lettered *THERE IS NO PLANET B* sign—complete with a wonky blue and green ball that only looked like Earth if you squinted generously enough—yelling for change, yelling for action, yelling because it made them feel strong and fierce and seen for once in their lives. And for what? For fucking *what?*

She kicks the bin. A coffee cup at the top of the pile teeters and falls to the grass below. She kicks the bin again, harder this time, feeling the metal reverberate beneath the sole of her booted foot. And again.

"What the hell do you think you're doing?"

The man is standing a couple of metres away, fists braced on his hips. He's about her dad's age, maybe older, and is wearing his blue disposable mask beneath his nose. In his hand is a takeaway coffee cup.

"What do you think *you're* doing?" Jinx shouts back.

His eyes narrow and he points to the rubbish that's tumbled from the bin. "Pick all that up, you little brat."

Jinx feels flushed, like when she's embarrassed, only this time she's really not. This time, the heat floods from a dark and livid well deep inside her, floods molten through her limbs until her hands are shaking and her teeth clench tight enough to crack. She wrenches off her own mask and marches up to the man.

"You pick it up," she yells at him. "It's your mess, you fucking pick it up. All of it. It's not my job to clean up after you, you ... *arsehole!"*

Alarmed, the man steps back a pace, muttering something that Jinx can't quite catch, although the words *crazy* and *bitch* manage to make it through the triple-ply. She swallows, all too aware now of the other people in the park, all of them staring straight at her. Nearby, a mother holds her little boy close to her legs, pushing the kid behind her like Jinx might be about to rush them next. Almost all the adults are wearing masks and it's unnerving how she can only see their eyes—or not, because so many of them have sunglasses on as well. It's like they're robots, or aliens. It's like that old movie that Tyler made them watch about the creepy pods that hatched things that looked just like you except they weren't, and Jinx wonders if the park people aren't all about to point at her and scream.

Her heart beats hard in her chest and Jinx just can't anymore. She sucks in a deep breath and yells at the man one last time, a wordless guttural roar that means everything and nothing and hollows her to a spent and brittle husk.

Then she runs.

There is the tiniest fraction of truth in the lemming-suicide myth, a seed from which the tales grew tall. They take things to extremes, those little rodents. Tundra-bound in winter, digging through the snow for buried grasses and moss, excavating a subterranean metropolis of tunnels and burrows and generally living the hardest of hardscrabble lives. Come spring, though, they're off to the high country to hang out among the trees and heath-patched plains, catch some rays and pretty much fuck so damn prolifically that every three or four years they reach critical mass, population wise. Too many lemmings, not enough food, not enough space, not enough of anything except more lemmings, and so off they go. Wave after furry wave they migrate, very nearly all of them dying along the way. Starvation, thirst, hypothermia, exhaustion and yeah, getting your throat torn open by your buddy over the last blade of cottongrass, or because he just doesn't like your face. You'd get tetchy too, resources stretched so slim and no promised land in sight. But enough of them survive, the species skimming extinction's edge but nevertheless managing to keep their grip, and the whole vicious cycle begins again. It'd be easier, you'd think, to simply keep things under control. To manage your shit with a little more finesse year to year and so avoid the very real risk you'll end up a forgotten, decomposing carcass on the road to nowhere in particular. But they're only lemmings. They can't see that far ahead.

Her old phone is almost fully charged by the time Jinx has nuked herself a cup of instant noodles—because her dad won't let her slink back to her room without taking something to eat with her and the microwave is quicker than arguing. Sitting on her bed, she slurps wet carbs into her mouth with a fork while she waits out the interminable updates, signing in to the most vital apps, putting her notifications on silent. The vid has already been pulled from TikTok but who cares when it's been copied and uploaded to any number of places since. Her friends have been passing new links around like swap cards; nothing online ever dies.

Jinx puts in her earbuds, glances up to make sure her door is closed. Taps play.

It starts with sky blue, a wisp of clouds, then pans swiftly down to a boy who looks maybe a year or two older than her. Dark, shaggy hair and a smile that wobbles at the edges. Angry rash of acne along his jawbone but still cute, in a sort of K-Pop way, if K-Pop boys could ever give up their filters. Wherever he is, it's windy and behind him, around him, are the tops of tall buildings. He's high, wherever he is. He's really high.

We are the virus, he says. The wind snips the edges of his words. *And we are also the cure.*

Another smile that stretches a beat too long, that looks scared and certain and about as wrong as a smile can look and—

—he jumps. No, falls. No, *lets* himself fall. Backwards and over and down and it's so fast it can't be real, must be staged, some clever trick and the boy is going to leap up from the bottom of the frame any second and yell, *fooled you suckers!*

Except the camera was so steady, leaning forward over the edge to track the descent as its subject flailed and grew smaller and—stopped.

It wasn't a selfie. Someone was holding that phone, up on the rooftop with the boy, knowing what he was planning to do the whole time. Probably the same person who uploaded the vid in the first place.

Jinx's cheeks are hot.

She taps replay. Because there's something ... right at the end ... there: when the boy lands (dies), you can't see it clearly through the burst of pixels that's been put in over the top. A minor explosion of blue, green and white, like a tiny cartoon firework ... *replay*: that sound, another digital manipulation edited in post, and she knows that sound.

She *knows* it. Jinx replays the last few seconds. And again.

It's from the game. The noise a lemming makes when it falls too far to land safely, that weird computerised *squish* that sounds remarkably akin to something very soft hitting something very, very hard. The explosion is from the game as well—the primitive pixel spray of lemming meeting ground. Someone took it all and edited it into this vid. To obscure the worst? To be funny? What kind of sick fuck thinks it's cool to make a joke of this?

Jinx replays the vid, again and again until her stomach threatens to send back the noodles, express service, no signature required.

"Okay," she whispers. "Enough now."

There are dozens of alerts and notifications all over her apps, messages from Cazz and Tyler and a bunch of group chats with randoms from school who've tagged her in the general frenetic buzz of *OMG* and *WTF* and *have you seen?*

A fresh DM pops up from Cazz who must've noticed she's back online.

whats up with all this shit??

yeah, Jinx messages back, *its fucked. that poor kid*

which one??

which what?

Over the next hour or so they find eight more. Different kids, different cities and times of day, but otherwise a terrible familiarity to them all. *We are the virus. And we are also the cure.* The same pixelated explosion as they hit the pavement, the grass, the water, the body already sprawled broken on the ground. The same squishy sound effect that seems less and less ridiculous the more Jinx hears it. *We are the virus. And we are also the cure.* Another handful by the time her dad knocks on the door to say that dinner is ready and Jinx shoves the phone under her pillow in case he comes in and confiscates it as well.

She eats as much of the home-delivered green curry as she can manage, which isn't much at all, and mumbles something about not feeling well when her dad notices.

He throws her a sharp glance, reaches out to touch her face. "Fever?"

Jinx flinches. "Jesus, it's not COVID, okay? I'm just not hungry."

He lets her go back to her room. Where she curls up beneath her doona and searches and taps and swipes until she can barely keep her eyes open. Until all she can see when she closes them is that fucking pixelated explosion. There are so many, mostly kids around her age give or take a couple of years but a couple of people who looked like they were in their twenties maybe. It's trending on Twitter and Facebook too. It's trending everywhere. Jinx keeps searching.

We are the virus. And we are also the cure.

Replay.

The lemmings in the game, they're organised. *Organisable* at least. Climbing, building, digging, bashing, floating—together they command a skill set that will see the whole tribe through the deadly array of obstacles and safely home. Most of them, anyway. Most of the time. Not the blockers, who plant themselves with arms outstretched, foot tapping in refusal as they shake their heads back and forth. *No. You shall not pass. There be dragons ... or acid, or lava or a fall from which you won't recover. Turn back, stay safe*. And the other lemmings do, and they are. You'd think, wouldn't you, that the blockers would get to go home too? Once their job is done and all their buddies are successfully warned away, they could simply *unblock* and bring up the rear. But once a blocker, forever a blocker, holding the line until the clock runs down to zero. Unless you get bored of waiting and make them a bomber instead—the other specialist who won't ever see a warm burrow again. 5-4-3-2-1: POP! Five tiny white pixels be all that's left of those dudes. Blasting a necessary access point can be the only way through sometimes and they take up the mantle so readily. Hunkered down, hands on head as they shudder and shake, beeping out a tinny *Oh no!* just before they explode. It's cute, if you don't think too hard about it. But if you do think about it—all those stoic little blockers and bombers sacrificing themselves to warn the others, to forge an escape route they can never, ever take—then you might see things differently. They're *brave*, those lemmings. The bravest collection of pixels to ever grace a screen.

At 6:18 a.m. the multi-storey parking lot at the shopping centre is all but deserted. A handful of cars on the ground floor, spaced out and shadowed in thin dawn light, and it's one of the creepiest things Jinx has seen. Post-apocalyptic. The stairwell smells bad, rancid with stale piss. She pulls the collar of her shirt over her nose as she hauls herself up the several flights to the roof. It's hard work on so little sleep.

Out here the air is clear, crisp with the chill of early winter, and Jinx sucks it deep into her lungs. She's never paid attention to the view before: the surrounding suburbs unfolding around her, the roads eerily empty of commuter traffic. A few people are out running or walking their dogs but they all look so small and distant, like they're not really part of the world. Or like Jinx isn't.

"Hey!"

The girl is sitting against the wall of the cark park, tucked into the corner opposite the stairwell. She pushes herself to her feet as Jinx approaches, tucks her curly brown hair behind her ears. Her t-shirt is bright pink with a unicorn across the chest. Its mane and tail are painted with rainbow glitter.

"Hey," Jinx echoes, offering a timid wave.

The girl looks her up and down, eyes narrowed. "We are the virus?"

Jinx pauses. "Oh, right. And we are also the cure."

The girl with the unicorn shirt nods. "I was wondering if anyone else would think of this place."

"Yeah." Jinx looks over the edge of the railing to the entrance below. Empty bitumen, a clear line of sight. "It's pretty high."

"High enough anyway. A few good seconds, right?"

Jinx leans back, rubs her upper arms.

The girl is holding out her iPhone. It looks like a new model. Expensive, encased in bling. "Have you done this before? Filmed, I mean? Obviously."

Jinx shakes her head.

"Okay, no probs. I'm signed in to everything you'll need." She spends a few minutes walking Jinx through. How to record and save, how to find the sound file and filter, how to edit, how to upload and tag and share, and even though Jinx knows almost all of it already, she lets the girl tell her, lets her tell her twice even. "Got it?

"Got it?"

"You sure? There won't be a second take."

"I got it." Gently, Jinx takes the phone from the girl's outstretched hand. "Do you think … do you think this will work? Do you think it will make any difference?"

The girl shrugs and climbs up onto the railing. "At least we're doing something. And a few less people in the world can't be bad thing, you know." She swings a leg over the top, spreads her arms wide. "You feel it, right? The connection? Being a part of something bigger than just yourself? Maybe if more people felt like that we wouldn't be here."

"Maybe," Jinx whispers. She steps up to the railing, phone ready.

"Hey." The girl grabs Jinx by the wrist, her dilated pupils as flat as drops of oil on a garage floor. "You're not going to flake, are you? I've heard that's happened. You know, like, people not filming, dropping the phone. Or not posting after."

"I got you," Jinx says. "Promise."

And she does. Keeping the girl centre frame as she speaks her final lines, following her descent all the way down. It's so fast, Jinx's hands only start to shake as she's editing the clip, making sure the little burst of pixels cover the girl's legs, the broken way they twist on the bitumen, and also the halo that glistens and seeps from beneath her head.

Once the video is posted, Jinx sinks to the ground. She switches off the screen and leans the phone against the concrete wall. She never asked the girl what she should do with it, after. Never even asked the girl her name. Jinx closes her eyes. Her hands aren't shaking anymore and maybe she can feel it, a million fragile filaments stretching out from her fingertips and into the world, snaking and sparking their way through the air, through Wi-Fi and Bluetooth and data driven on currents of 5G, seeking connection and, finding it, calling them all to arms. Calling them all home.

The hinges on the stairwell door screech and Jinx looks over as a boy in a grey beanie steps onto the roof. He sees her and raises a hand, more in salute than a wave, then starts towards where she's sitting.

Jinx pulls her phone from her pocket. She can't really describe it, the calmness spreading through her body. It's not that she isn't scared, but still. It's like there's a very thin, very strong cord anchored in her sternum, guiding her forward. Gently. Firmly. She's never been more sure of anything.

Holding the phone up to her face, she presses record. "Dad? I love you, okay? You're not … this isn't your fault." The boy in the beanie is close now. "Don't watch, okay? Please don't watch." She stops recording, texts it to her dad.

The boy has stopped a couple of metres away. "Um, hi."

Jinx straightens, swipes at an errant tear. The cord in her chest tightens and tugs. Taking a deep breath, she holds the boy's gaze. His eyes are green, bright as bottle-glass and just as hard. Jinx holds out her phone.

"We are the virus."

And we are also the cure. And we are also the cure.

And

we

are

also

the

cure.

THE MACABRE READER

LYSETTE STEVENSON

THE SHADOW BOOK **OF JI YUN: THE CHINESE CLASSIC OF WEIRD TRUE TALES, HORROR STORIES AND OCCULT KNOWLEDGE** by Ji Yun translated by Yi Izzy Yu and John Yu Branscum. Cover based on Odilon Redon's *Everywhere Eyeballs are Aflame*.

Ji Yun was the Imperial Librarian, Head of the Department of War and was a close confidant to the royal emperor. With records starting in 1789, Ji Yun collected five volumes of supernatural phenomena from the surrounding villages. Each of the entries are only about two to four pages long and written matter-of-factly like a dossier. Yi Izzy Yu and John Yu take a modern approach to the translation, lending the work a contemporary voice that brings out the weird with the comically absurd.

It's a veritable cornucopia of bizarre and cosmic horrors that transport you to a fog-shrouded countryside, where trans-dimensional beings are commonplace, ghosts caterwaul from haunted trees and the living are stalked by the dead. Specters are plentiful alongside trickster foxes, amorous tree spirits and Tibetan black magicians as rural superstitions mix readily with Taoist mysticism. Much of the humour comes through in the way these impossible occurrences are viewed as little more than daily nuisances by the narrators of each tale.

Clocking in at eighty-two vignettes, this collection opens the reader up to seeing the world in a whole new way. Thrilling us with possibilities of the uncanny and the horror of discovering realms beyond our small grasp of consciousness.

The Sorcerer's Apprentice: Tales and Conjurations by Charles Johnson. Cover Illustration by Keith Piper.

Charles R. Johnson is a writer and scholar that needs no introduction but is not commonly associated with the horror genre. That said, the short stories in *The Sorcerer's Apprentice* show homages to Mary Shelley's Frankenstein, UFO encounters, pulp noir and martial arts fandom. A curse, following a break and enter that could as easily be found in the pages of EC comics as it did in this highly acclaimed, PEN Faulkner nominated, collection.

The storyteller's ease throughout makes the moments of surrealism and horror more impactful, while centering the philosophical questions around class, race, and the black experience in America. A philosophy professor is taken down a phantasmagorical rabbit hole by a student in a black housing project. A country doctor is abducted by a spaceship in need of his services. Animals in a pet store revolt when the owner fails to return. Two young boys creep about in the dark of their elderly neighbour's home. A farm hand is molded into his boss's likeness. The titular story sees the process of magical initiation fail with disastrous consequences.

These allegorical stories bring up issues of midlife crisis and transformation, of class struggle post slavery and free will vs self-determination. The horror and menace is visceral as the tension ratchets. A melding of genres by an undoubtedly talented writer makes this a rich and fantastic collection.

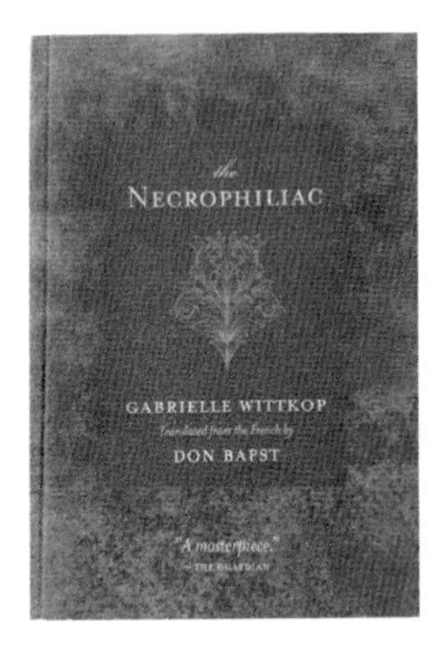

The Necrophiliac by Gabrielle Wittkop, translated from French by Don Bapst.

Written as diary entries into the personal life of Lucien, a bachelor necrophile. Gabrielle Wittkop creates a protagonist and a sensory experience that pushes up against every transgression. A petite novella so decadent and depraved you honestly wouldn't want anything longer.

Set in Paris with its sprawling cemeteries this is a meditation on the essence of love and desire; examined through the intense one-way passion of the necrophile. Despite this Wittkop succeeds in drawing a sympathetic portrait of Lucien, an antique dealer, dapper, composed and somewhat handsome though off-putting and often smelling like a miasma of decay. A connoisseur of his desires, whether male or female, old or very young, he records every passionate detail as the rigor mortis sets and wanes. Lucien is so consumed by lust for the next sexual conquest, he leaves Paris for an extended holiday in Naples, a metropolis he affectionately describes as "the most macabre of cities." Through his diary we experience his trials and tribulations, his encounters and opinions of other ghouls and his ultimately unsuccessful attempts in trying to maintain the corpses he loves for as long and as inconspicuous as possible. You can't help but feel for how lonely and fleeting the nature of Lucien's affairs are.

While incredibly morbid with its attention to detail, blackened humour and for crossing every last possible taboo; it is also a poetic and beautifully rendered character study, you won't soon forget.

The Accursed by Claude Seignolle. Translated from French by Bernard Wall, with a foreword by Lawrence Durrell.

Claude Seignolle, a master storyteller and folklorist, spent his life gathering oral traditions from the French countryside, particularly its supernatural mysteries. *The Accursed* contains two superb novellas of diabolical folk horror.

In the first tale, *Malvenue*, we encounter a petulant young farm girl and her coming of age during the wheat harvest. Prior to her birth, the marshes surrounding the farmland were believed by the locals to be haunted. Despite this, her father stubbornly ploughs the allegedly cursed field and disturbs a relic of an earlier pagan god. As the daughter uncovers a piece of the relic hidden in the woods, a malevolent and dangerous power overcomes her.

The second novella, *Maria the Wolf*, similarly features a young girl coming into her sexual prowess. As an infant Maria is visited by a wolf drover, who tells her family she was born with special healing abilities and the gift of communicating with wolves. In a village where the threat of werewolves stalks the night, the utterance from this visitor is akin to a malediction. As she comes of age, suspicion over her lithe physique and sulphurous eyes, turns her village against her.

Seignolle's talent as a writer is on full display here. The eldritch atmosphere and high stakes pacing in each of these tales is perfect. To read *The Accursed* is to immerse yourself in an unearthly countryside filled with all manner of spectral menace, old gods and bewitchment.

Daemon in Lithuania by Henri Guigonnat. Translated from French by Barbara Wright. Cover and inside illustrations by Erica Weihs.

In the late 1960's Henri Guigonnat was part of Parisian bohemia. After being invited by surrealist painter Leonora Fini to an artistic getaway on the island of Corsica, Henri became bored and set to the task of writing. Though Daemon in Lithuania was lauded throughout the French literary community on its publication in 1973, this was his only book.

More neo-gothic fabulism than pulp horror, nonetheless Guigonnat's storytelling breathes such macabre charm it's like an Edward Gorey drawing come to life. You meet an eccentric and reclusive extended family living amidst a Carpathian-like mountain range of Lithuania. Their lives are changed when an exceptional cat is discovered living in the castle's attic. The cat soon has a profound effect on each member of the family as they seek to appease its every whim. The cat becomes the family's daemon, a spirited familiar whose very presence brings to the surface the inner secrets of everyone who comes near it. As their love for it grows so too does the Daemon's body grow grander by the day.

Even with its light-hearted and comedic tone, this horror novel ranges from bloodletting with exploding leeches to scenic cemetery walks and candle lit dinner parties amidst storms howling off the mountain side. There are vampires, shapeshifters, and a possibility the cat's expanding girth has something to do with the missing village children. Daemon in Lithuania is a joyfully goth and absurdist read.

THE MIND THING by Fredric Brown. Cover illustrated by George Underwood.

A malefic alien, exiled by its home planet, is randomly beamed to the farmlands of Wisconsin. Though a highly intelligent being, the gravitational field of earth makes its turtle-like shell incapable of movement. Its advantage is in its ability to psychically inhabit the mind of any human, animal or bird that sleeps within close proximity to it. Observing the possibilities life on earth could provide to its species, the Mind Thing's mission is to control the body of a human that will be able to transmit it back to its home planet. Once there it can gather an alliance and return to invade earth.

The caveat to releasing itself from the mind it is occupying is that the host must die. As the parasitic alien furthers it's goal, the surrounding area experiences what appears to be a mass hysteria of suicide among both man and animal. The Mind Thing uses and discards each of its hosts as it closes in on its target, a physics professor on sabbatical in an isolated farmhouse.

Fast paced, pulpy, ironic and nasty. With a cast of unconventional and fleshed out characters that make the tension of their fates so much the worse, and an ending that captures the essence of cosmic horror. This is Fredric Brown writing earthbound sci-fi-horror at its best.

Doctor Arnoldi by Tiffany Thayer. Cover illustrated by Gavin O'Keefe.

Tiffany Thayer was an actor, founder of the Fortean Society and a popular genre writer of the thirties. This foray into apocalyptic horror with Doctor Arnoldi shocked fans and critics alike. The original print run had a striking cover and overleaf with a floating river of nude golden bodies. It is uncommon and highly collectable but the late Richard Lupoff of Ramble House press, so taken with the bizarreness of Doctor Arnoldi brought it back into print as an affordable paperback and a cover, that lacks the art deco elegance of the original but is oddly fitting in its own way.

The year is 1930 and people have suddenly stopped dying. No matter how horrific the accident, the body keeps twitching. Funeral homes and mortuaries are empty. Bodies soon fill the hospitals and streets as the conundrum of what to do when the dead are not really dead overwhelms communities across North America.

The titular character Doctor Arnoldi is a mysterious and infamous old Russian doctor living on the third floor of a low rent New York apartment. Befriended by the journalist who first broke the story and his neighbour, a young woman whose husband was one of the early victims of this new phenomena, they try to figure out what is happening while the steadfast Doctor Arnoldi seems to understand more than he ever lets on. Heavily inspired by the 1913 nihilistic novel Breaking Point by Russian author Mikhail Artsybashev, Thayer succeeds in producing his own grisly and theatrical fever dream.

Bearwalk by Tom Peltier & Lynne Sallot. Cover illustrated by Norval Morrisseau.

Based on true events from Tom Peltier's life, Lynne Sallot helped co-write a fictional narrative around the Ojibwe belief in Bearwalkers. A bearwalker is someone who has taken an oath to black magic. A shaman who uses evil to wreak havoc in the pursuit of vengeance and power.

Set in Northern Michigan, an indigenous lawyer, raised by a white family away from his reservation, returns to his community to help fight a case for land rights. His wife, who is also the daughter to the reservation's chief, and their two children join him during his stay at the family home. What was thought to be a working summer, using his skills to help and reconnect with his culture, also reignites the ancestral bearwalk curse.

Writers in the 1980s horror boom frequently appropriated indigenous culture and beliefs. Here Tom Peltier lets the reader into the roles of medicine men, vision quests, and the traditions and practices around Animism. When the horror hits it is no less terrifying and no one is safe. Written over forty years ago it deals with the still prevalent issues of racism and profiling as the indigenous lawyer navigates between these two worlds. This book is so cinematic in its telling, it's a wonder it still hasn't been translated into film.

Tom Peltier was an active member in Canadian politics and

founder of The Manitou Island Arts Foundation along with luminaries Daphne Odjig and Carl Ray. He was fundamental in promoting indigenous arts and culture in Canada and abroad. *Bearwalk* was his only book.

CONTRIBUTORS

Oluwatomiwa Ajeigbe is a writer of the dark and fantastical, a poet and a reluctant mathematician. He has poetry and fiction published or forthcoming from *The Magazine of Fantasy and Science Fiction, Fantasy Magazine, Baffling Magazine, Lightspeed Magazine* and elsewhere. When he's not writing about malfunctioning robots or crazed gods, he can be found doing whatever people do on Twitter at @OluwaSigma. He writes from a room with broken windowpanes in Lagos, Nigeria.

J.T. Bundy lives in London with his partner and a neurotic cat. His short fiction has previously appeared in *Idle Ink,* and he's currently working on his first novel.

William Curnow lives in London. His stories have been published in various places, including *Supernatural Tales, Egaeus Press,* and *Jurassic London.*

Brian Evenson is the author of over a dozen works of fiction, most recently *The Glassy, Burning Floor of Hell.* His collection *Song for the Unraveling of the World* won the World Fantasy Award and the Shirley Jackson Award, and was a Ray Bradbury Prize finalist. His novel *Last Days* won the ALA-RUSA award for Best Horror novel of 2009. His novel *The Open Curtain* was a finalist for an Edgar Award and his collection *The Wavering Knife* won the International Horror Guild Award. He is the recipient of three O. Henry Prizes, an NEA fellowship, and a Guggenheim Award. His work has been translated into more than a dozen languages. He lives in Los Angeles and teaches at CalArts.

Orrin Grey is a skeleton who likes monsters as well as the author of several spooky books. His stories of ghosts, monsters, and sometimes the ghosts of monsters can be found in dozens of anthologies, including Ellen Datlow's *Best Horror of the Year*. He resides in the suburbs of Kansas City and watches lots of scary movies. You can visit him online at orringrey.com.

Vince Haig is an illustrator, designer, and author. You can visit Vince at his website: barquing.com

Dan Howarth is a writer from the North of England. Dan is the author of the short story collection *Dark Missives* and the snowbound horror novella, *Territory*. His debut novel *Lionhearts* also hit the shelves from Grey Matter Press in 2022. Dan's short fiction has featured in numerous places, namely The Other Stories podcast where his stories have been downloaded over 100,000 times. Dan was shortlisted for a Debut Novel Award by New Writing North in 2021. Dan's website is www.danhowarthwriter.com

Our cover artist, **Barandash Karandashich**, is from Moscow, and works in pencil, ink, water-colour, and digital painting.

Kirstyn McDermott has been working in the darker alleyways of speculative fiction for much of her career. She is the author of two award-winning novels, *Madigan Mine* and *Perfections*, and a collection of short fiction, *Caution: Contains Small Parts*. Her stories and poetry have been published in various magazines, journals and anthologies both within Australia and internationally, with her most recent work being *Never Afters*, a series of novellas that retell classic fairy tales. She holds a PhD in creative writing with a research focus on re-visioned fairy tales and produces and co-hosts a literary discussion podcast, *The Writer and the Critic*. Kirstyn lives in Ballarat, Australia, with fellow writer Jason Nahrung and two distinctly non-literary felines. She can be found online at www.kirstynmcdermott.com.

Interior artist **Dan Rempel** is an illustrator from Lawrence, KS who likes to create images that evoke mood and a sense of narrative. He is especially drawn to depicting scenes of imagination, mystery, adventure, and the macabre. Visit danrempelillustration.com to see more of his work.

Richard Strachan lives in Edinburgh, UK. He has had short fiction published in magazines like *Interzone, The Lonely Crowd, Gutter* and *New Writing Scotland,* and has also published a number of novels and stories for Games Workshop's Black Library imprint.

Lysette Stevenson is a stage manager with a rural outdoor equestrian theatre company and a second generation bookseller. She lives in British Columbia.

Simon Strantzas is the author of five collections of short fiction, including *Nothing is Everything* (Undertow Publications, 2018), and editor of a number of anthologies, including *Year's Best Weird Fiction, Vol. 3.* Combined, he's been a finalist for four Shirley Jackson Awards, two British Fantasy Awards, and the World Fantasy Award. His fiction has appeared in numerous annual best-of anthologies, and in venues such as *Nightmare, The Dark,* and *Cemetery Dance*. In 2014, his edited anthology, *Aickman's Heirs,* won the Shirley Jackson Award. He lives with his wife in Toronto, Canada.

Megan Taylor is the author of four dark novels, *How We Were Lost, The Dawning, The Lives of Ghosts,* and *We Wait,* as well as a collection of short stories, *The Woman Under the Ground*. Further short stories have been placed in several competitions and appeared in a variety of journals and anthologies, including the *Dark Lane* anthologies, *Neon,* and *The Invisible Collection* (Nightjar Press). For more information, please visit www.megantaylor.info

Charlotte Turnbull's fiction has won prizes and appeared in *Litro, Barren Magazine,* and *Denver Quarterly,* among others. Her work has been Pushcart-nominated, and translated into Italian. She was long-listed for the 2022 Caledonia Prize, and lives on Dartmoor with her husband and three children.

Zachariah Claypole White is currently pursuing an MFA in poetry at Sarah Lawrence College. Previously, he managed the independent bookstore, Flyleaf Books, in Chapel Hill, North Carolina. He graduated from Oberlin College in 2017, with a major in creative writing and a minor in English literature. His poetry and prose have appeared in numerous publications, including *The Raven Review*, *Scalawag*, and *The Hong Kong Review*. He won *Flying South*'s 2021 Best in Category award for poetry and his work has been nominated for a Pushcart Prize. Zachariah uses writing to navigate his lifelong struggle with anxiety, depression, and OCD.

WEIRD
HORROR

WEIRD HORROR MAGAZINE

AUTUMN 2022

ISSUE 5

EDITED BY

MICHAEL KELLY

WEIRD HORROR 5
Autumn 2022

PUBLISHER
Undertow Publications
Pickering, Canada

EDITOR / LAYOUT
Michael Kelly

PROOFREADER
Carolyn Macdonell

OPINION
Simon Strantzas

COMMENTARY
Orrin Grey

BOOKS
Lysette Stevenson

COVER ART
Barandash Karandashich

COVER DESIGN
Vince Haig

INTERIOR ART
Dan Rempel

https://www.weirdhorrormagazine.com